PATH OF LIFE
JOURNAL

PATH OF LIFE
JOURNAL

JULIE GEDDES

To order additional copies of this book, contact:
Xlibris Corporation
1-888-795-4274
www.Xlibris.com
Orders@Xlibris.com
101808

CONTENTS

DEDICATION

I Wrote this book for my counselling practice—it can be used as a Quick Reference Guide for everyone along the path of life.

The young girl is looking into a waterfall and daydreaming about what her life will be. She see herself in the mist of the water and below is her path.

Sketch Artist: Arida Douglas

FRIEND

Hold fast to your dreams
Within your heart
Keep one still, secret spot
Where dreams may go,
And Sheltered so, may strive and grow.
Where doubt and fear are not
O' Keep a place apart
Within your heart, for little dreams to go!

Author: Micheal Dalton

A. QUICK REFERENCE

Individual strain = Relationships under strain

It is my belief and hope that this book will teach us all to be better in communications/ counselling with one another and self.

MY THEORY

Applicable for each "S" Word along the path of life
Foundational Spiritual Theory with a person-centered
relationship and integrative techniques.
Julie Geddes (R.P.C.)(C.P.C.A.)
Path of Life Private Counselling.

1. **WE ALL NEED TO SHARE OUR STORY**

   IT IS VITAL TO RECEIVE UNCONDITIONAL REGARD
   when we share our life path with another. THIS
   ACKNOWLEDGEMENT IS VITAL RESPECT and helps
   one resolve feelings and heals thought patterns.

   Our very life depends on everything recurring 'til we answer
   from within." Robert Frost"

   I USE THE "S" WORD SCALE WHEN COUNSELLING to
   access your situational awareness.

   **Sick, Sorrowing, Suffering, Struggling,Starving,
   Sinning, Searching,Suicidal, Sad, Scared, Stressed
   and those who SERVE.**

2. **WE ALL HAVE SPIRITUAL AGENCY**

   Use Gift of AGENCY = Individual Responsibility
   THINK FEEL ACT = FAITH HOPE CHARITY
   We are free to become AWARE/CHOOSE/CREATE—how
   we view our subjective reality or world.
   We are free according to our capacity for self-awareness to
   gain knowledge.

We are free to learn, serve, grow UNDERSTANDING SELF/ Developing Goals/ Healthy Skills

No matter what happens to us we do not have to ACCEPT it as a defining factor.

3. WE ALL NEED SUPPORT ALONG THE WAY/TIME NEEDED

To know we are loved and cared for and where we come from is a vital basic need.

WE ARE DUAL BEINGS:

- One is temporal/physical needs which allows us such opportunity of life.
- The other is Akin to the Divine Spiritual=HOW WE THINK FEEL ACT

look at each one seperately

1. **thoughts**
2. **feelings**
3. **actions**

    THIS IS YOUR SPIRIT = YOU

Along the Path of Life we can feel distress especially as we start out on our own!

I believe that LOSS is the trigger of the "S" words SICK SORROWING SUFFERING STRUGGLING STARVING SINNING SEARCHING SUICIDAL SAD SCARED STRESSED AND SERVING (12)

1. Remember there is no place for "BLAME" when we experience the "S" Words along the path of life.
2. Everyone is different even though same "S" and to reach out for individual help is a sign of great STRENGTH.
3. Not only can we use this theory for communicating with others but GIVING IT TO OURSELF IS ALSO VITAL. This is a good guide to loving yourself. Maturity is thus.
4. Some of the best Counsellors are those who have or are going through tough times because they will truly know to understand and succor.
5. Never Disown anyone that is damaging to all involved. The thing to do is limit contact as much as needed at the time.

(1) SICK

MY COMMENT: Endowed with agency, we are agents, and we primarily are to act and not merely be acted upon—especially as we "seek learning . . . by study and also by faith" (D&C 88:118).

This also apply's for other things like Healing Others—for example. As individuals we need to exercise our faith in asking and seeking out the Blessing for ourselves. When others think they can call down the Lord to Heal someone too often—they are taking away the agency and chance for others to act for themselves.

As gospel learners, we should be "doers of the word, and not hearers only" (James 1:22).

One LOSS can bring about other losses along the path of life.

There certainly can be many times when we feel sad even guilty . . . that we cannot do things with our loved ones we want to do.

Times when SICKNESS may play a huge part. It may cause strain on our relationships. No one wants this to happen or planned on having such a chore. These things make or break us. Sometimes it feels like its broke us. Our hearts will be burned through the fire to refine our spirits. Thoughts, Feelings, Actions. Making these three things become one. If I were to share one thing of wisdom that has come to my spirit in suffering these things it would be this:

None of us go through this alone it affects those around us.

The last thing we want is for our loved ones to suffer. So, we try our best to hide it. The parts we cannot hide often bring about suffering in the relationships we have because no one is perfect and even though they are supporting us the best they can it can be frustrating by times not to be able to help or fix and understand why.

REMEMBER WHEN YOU ARE THE ONE THAT IS SICK:

Others will by times take it out on things they should'nt—maybe even you. Try not to take their actions to heart—have a soft answer and forgive quickly. Be assertive when you need to to teach if that is what is needed. Following up with a greater expression of your love for them.

This is extremely hard to do when you are the one ill. Time apart also may have to be the appropriate thing until the loved one settles down. It is extremely damaging to express your deep fears to a loved one who is sick because that is the one thing they count on is you to be there for them. This is where each individuals faith and a trustworthy friend and the community services are of such value.

If your SICKNESS is causing your family strain and they are fighting often over it—even blaming your for their frustrations.

I would suggest that you use my "Contract Idea"found in this book. This can be used in many different situations. Remember it takes time for acceptance to come for all kinds of LOSS.

Helping Family Understand and Support the Chronic Pain Patient

This Article was written by my dear IC Sister Dawn Elder Kelly

HELPING FAMILY UNDERSTAND AND SUPPORT THE CHRONIC PATIENT BY DAWN ELDER KELLY

When I first thought about how I wanted to write this article, I nearly panicked. I thought as a chronic pain patient myself, "Holy cow!!! I don't even know where to start because I don't get most of the support that I need from my own family at this point, so how am I going to help others get the support that they need?" Then it hit me, what better way to help others in chronic pain than by expressing what I need in forms of support from my family and also by sharing the experiences I have had with the individuals in my life who have been ignorant to chronic pain and who have just flat out refused to try to accept it or learn more about it in order to help support me over the years. I know for a fact that all chronic pain patients have gone through tough times with their families to some extent. Its important that they all know they're not alone! Not getting the support that I need has only fueled me to find out more about the things that I do need from my family in order for me to continue this battle on a daily basis while having healthy relationships with them.

My Chronic Pain Experience In a Nutshell

Ten years ago, I developed chronic daily persistent headaches with intermittent migraines for no apparent reason. On top of having daily head pain, three years ago I was diagnosed with a painful bladder disease called Interstitial Cystitis. I ended up losing my bladder due to the disease, but I then developed a different type of chronic pelvic pain due to complications from the surgery. As if I wasn't feeling bad enough physically, I was told by a couple family members that I stressed my mom out so bad as she tried to help me get better, that I was responsible for her getting cancer and for her losing her life. That was the toughest thing I have ever had to swallow and I still haven't fully recovered from those words. I thought, "how in the world could they actually say something like that to me?"It was because they chose not to invest any time in educating themselves about my conditions to better understand what a day with my pain is actually like for me.A second personal example for me, recently I was told that I have done nothing but "take advantage of my husband" since we've been married because I haven't been able to work the past several years and he has had to help with many things at home when I am unable to do them.I've also been told that "I made the choice to have chronic pain" and that "I should just tough it out".Last but certainly not least, being told "well, you look great, so you must not be hurting that bad!" it certainly not a compliment!So the question is, how do we help our families understand and support us? Its not as simple as pointing the finger and saying, "Well you need to do this and you need to do that." I've learned that we as chronic pain sufferers have responsibilities to fulfill as well. If our families see that we are doing everything we can to physically and emotionally be well, it may be easier to get them to do their part.

The Physical and Emotional Effects That Occur When Pain Becomes Chronic

For everyone seeking relief from chronic pain, other people in their lives are inevitably affected. This includes husbands and wives, parents and children, friends, employers, and coworkers. Chronic pain can interfere with every aspect of a person's life from work to relationships, to one's self esteem and emotional well being. When the injury or disease first begins, family and friends are often there to help the pain patient offering all kinds of support.But as the pain starts to persist for weeks, to months, to years, family and friends often become withdrawn, resentful, judgmental, frustrated, angry, and emotionally exhausted. These negative responses are often heightened as the pain patient withdrawals themselves from society with a complete sense of hopelessness and helplessness. As with many pain patients, there is a stigma attached. We are often told that the pain isn't real, that it's all in our heads, or that we're faking it to take advantage of others and to get sympathy. Saying such things further drops the pain patient into a downward spiral of hopelessness and magnifies the existing pain syndrome. The misjudgments and assumptions made by others also complicate the anxiety and depression a lot of pain patients have developed due to the constant pain.

Communication Must Go Both Ways

The most important component to a healthy pain family is . . . COMMUNICATION! Family members need to hear from the pain patient what they need in terms of support and the family members need to express their feelings with the person in pain so that the communication is going both ways. Pain patients often feel like they have to carry the burden of proof, that it's not psychosomatic and they truly are in pain. They are often misunderstood because there may not be an amputation, a cast, or any external "proof" of pain. This can lead to feelings of resentment and anger for the pain patient. There may also be a tremendous amount of guilt over medications, inability to contribute financially, and the inability to enjoy physical activities at times. In some cases family members think the pain patient is "working it", or faking their symptoms for other gains. In all of these situations, the person in pain must communicate, "You know, it's really not helpful to me to have you disregard my situation".The pain patient may also want to let family members know that they are free to ask him or her questions about their illness to clear up any doubts that they may be having. On the flip side, the family member may feel helpless because they can't relieve their loved one's pain and they may feel guilt for having negative feelings or thoughts or for expressing unsupportive words or actions. So its important for the family member to be upfront with the person in pain and admit any feelings of guilt or resentment and to discuss those feelings with him or her. Both individuals need to express their feelings openly and honestly with each other.If the pain patient's spouse or loved one has cut off all emotional support, which may include not being affectionate, not providing optimism when he or she is feeling their worst, shows no interest in how his or her appointments go, or shows no interest in learning about their condition to better understand it, the individual in pain needs to communicate to their loved one by saying "I feel as though you have become emotionally distant by not doing . . ." or "In order to better understand my condition and what I go through, would you be willing to educate yourself about my pain syndrome?" If the pain patient doesn't speak up, the spouse or family member usually doesn't think there is a problem from the pain person's standpoint. They often see it as a one way street where the pain patient and his or her actions resulting from the pain is the only problem in the relationship.If family members are feeling angry or frustrated because they feel the person in pain is not doing all he or she can, then they need to discuss this with the pain person. If the person in pain is truly doing the best he or she can, that needs to be conveyed. If the pain patient thinks there are things that he or she knows they can do better, they need to make every effort to do those things and tell their loved one that they will try harder. Sometimes this can be very overwhelming and difficult for the parties involved.It may be very beneficial to get involved with a pain psychologist who can help each individual understand the other's feelings and who can help educate the family on chronic pain. If nothing is said from either party, the anger, frustration, and assumptions will continue to build and the relationship will become unhealthy and toxic. Love, commitment, and mutual respect are how all parties involved need to cope with a chronic illness. Chronic pain patients need their families to be open minded and nonjudgmental.

The Enabling Family

There are families that disregard the pain patient, but there are also families that enable the person. Either end of the spectrum is unhealthy. If the person in pain states, "I'm going to get a drink", and the non pain family member says, "No, don't move I'll get it", the pain patient needs to make it clear that it's not helpful to do everything for them.The person experiencing the pain needs to do as many activities independently as possible. The healthy loved one should encourage activities in the relationship.

The Chronic Pain Patient's Physical Responsibilities For Increased Functioning

One of the pain patient's most important roles in his or her relationships with family and in their own recovery, is to focus on restoring function and reducing self limiting behaviors, or "pain behaviors". Often the person in pain thinks they can't do something because it will ultimately cause more pain. This is natural, however, there's a difference between hurting at the same level regardless of whether one is active or not active and doing something that will cause physical damage.With proper treatment modalities in combination, the pain patient can begin to figure out what they can do and what their true limitations are. They will begin to realize the value of engaging in activities even if it's going to hurt. Pacing their activities will ultimately make the person in pain feel better about themselves because they will ultimately be able to do more.If the chronic pain body is pushed to do too much at one time, more pain and exhaustion may be the result. Exercise and physical therapy are crucial aspects for strengthening the chronic pain body and for producing natural endorphins.The more there is pain, the more likely the person is to be inactive which leads to more pain and muscle weakness and atrophy. This cycle must be broken and will be very challenging for awhile, but will become easier as the body gets used to being active again despite having pain.But again, pacing activities is a must! When I say exercise, I don't mean to try to run a marathon! I am referring to light walking, housework, or whatever can be done to move your muscles!

Other Responsibilities That the Pain Patient Must Consider

The pain patient needs to focus on eating fresh whole food to obtain the vitamins needed to regenerate new cell growth. Another important issue is getting 15 minutes of sunshine a day or two hours of sunshine a week which will provide adequate amounts of vitamin D. It is a proven fact that those in chronic pain tend to have low levels of vitamin D. If sunshine is not an option, vitamin D supplementation is important.Chronic pain experiencers need to get plenty of restful sleep.A body in pain uses up vital energy that needs to be replenished through good sleep habits. If resources such as chiropractic care, massage therapy, or acupuncture are available, they are extra modalities that can be tried to get relief.Finding a passion whether it be through a hobby, writing, sports, work if possible, or volunteering is necessary for mental well-being.It gives the chronic pain patient a sense of fulfillment, purpose and is a source of joy and inspiration.Engaging in relaxation skills, prayer,or mindful meditation will also offer amazing results for the body and mind. Remember, stress goes to the weakest identifiable part of the body . . . and in the chronic pain body, its going to be the site or sites of the pain condition.Last but not least, the chronic pain body should be rid of opiate pain killers if at all possible. I know this is a debatable subject amongst those of us in pain. But the fact is, in the long run, chronic opiate use can actually cause hyperalgesia, or more pain, by lowering the body's threshold for pain sensations and depleting the body's natural endorphins. Tolerance also becomes an issue leading to higher and higher amounts of narcotics which then leads to more hyperalgesia. Stopping opiates will be the most challenging part of healing because it may take several weeks to several months for the body to return to it's baseline level of pain and the person's pain level will be heightened to a great degree during this time.This is the time when the pain patient will need extra support.Explaining to the family what will happen during this time frame is important so that they understand why things are temporarily worsening. After this period of hypersensitivity, other nonnarcotic pain medications will work better.The person in pain should also try to limit telling their loved ones how much pain they are in.They should try to talk about other things that aren't going to bring up negative feelings and that won't drive family away from them. This is a very difficult "pain behavior" to break, but with practice, it can be minimized greatly.By doing some or all of the above recommendations, the chronic pain patient is trying to do all they can to help save themselves and their relationships within their families. But it must be known by all parties, including the pain patient, that progress can take time.More time than anyone might expect.We can't rush recovery!

Positivity

It is so important that the person in pain surround themselves with positive people, places, and things. It's extremely difficult to think positively at times when one is in chronic pain.To overcome this, practice cognitive behavioral therapy. Learn to change maladaptive thinking and behaviors. Just knowing one is practicing healthy living creates positive thoughts. Again, the main topic of this article is helping family understand and support the loved one in chronic pain. Communicating feelings and education will help build healthy relationships within the chronic pain family. If there is a relationship thats needs to be repaired, the person in pain needs to step up to the plate and take the steps to amend it.If that's not possible because the other party refuses to educate themselves or refuses to try harder to offer support, then that must be accepted by the pain patient and the relationship must be terminated due to the toxicity it will create in the chronic pain body and mind.

Simple Ways To Encourage the Chronic Pain Patient

As I was doing my research, I came across a simple list of five ways to encourage someone living with an invisible pain condition.People in chronic pain may want to share the following statements with their families.

1. "It's always great to see you! I know it's quite a sacrifice for you."
2. "I don't know how you do it. Your courage amazes me!"
3. "Given all that you have gone through, your attitude is incredible!"
4. "I keep hoping for a miracle, but I love you no matter what."
5. "I wish you could feel half as great as you look."

Some other positive statements that I would find helpful are, "things will get better", "we are in this together", "you are so strong and you can make it through this!", and "You are doing a great job, I know this is difficult". What may be helpful to one person may not be for someone else. I encourage all chronic pain experiencers to find what works best for them and to communicate such examples to their loved ones.

Things NOT To Say To a Chronic Pain Patient

I also came across a list of ten things NOT to say to someone with an invisible pain condition.

1. "Must be nice to sleep all day."
2. "You're lucky you don't have to work."
3. "I can relate."
4. "Just take something."
5. "Just try harder."
6. "Just be positive."
7. "You just want attention."

8. "It's all in your head."
9. "It could be worse."
10. "But you look good!"

Some other things I'd like to add to the list are, "But you had surgery, therefore you should be fixed", "If you can go to the mall, you can get a job", "If you can exercise, you must not hurt that bad", "How can all the doctors you've seen be wrong?", and "You must be doing this for the drugs". If any of these negative connotations are conveyed to the chronic pain patient, he or she must let the person know that their comments are very belittling and hurtful. The non-pain loved one should also be asked to be more supportive and asked to educate themselves to grasp an understanding of the chronic pain person's condition and what a day is like for them. If they continue to be condescending and unsupportive, the relationship should be ended. For those who refuse to give an effort, I found the following quote to be helpful, "My disabling chronic pain is more real than your imaginary medical expertise!"

Helpful Pain Websites

There are several websites where chronic pain patients and family members can go to for information.

I will include some of the general pain sites that are out there. I recommend that all pain patients also do their own research for sites that specifically deal with their particular disorders so that they can share them with their families to help them better understand what the person in pain is experiencing.Some websites are:

1. The American Chronic Pain Association—www.theacpa.org
2. The National Pain Foundation—www.nationalpainfoundation.org
3. The Chronic Pain Site—www.chronicpainsite.com
4. American Pain Society—www.ampainsoc.org
5. www.pain.com

Conclusion

We as chronic pain patients need to do what's best for us in all situations.That includes taking care of ourselves the best way possible, physically and mentally, and helping our families to be more supportive and understanding. We can only do our parts. The rest is up to them!We can't change what has happened to us and we certainly didn't ask for it. All we can do is move forward and live one day at a time as best we can! There is a life out there to enjoy despite having chronic pain! We can have that second chance in life if we choose to take the necessary steps in all aspects of our lives.Be strong my fellow pain survivors and NEVER give up!

Dawn Kelly, MA, NCC, LPC

TALKING TO CHILDREN AND YOUTH
When its time to talk about Chronic Illness

Emily Muir Redd : Julie, do you do this online professionally?? Awesome..how much do u charge an hour? Counsel people w/ chronic disease/pain or other stuff too? I think it would be so healthy for the entire family to get counseling when a member of family has a chronic disease. I wish I knew better how to talk to my kids about it.

Talking to Children and Youth
When it's time to discuss a family member's chronic illness

When illness affects a family, the children—including the offspring or siblings of people with mental illness—are just as confused and scared as the adult family members. They know something is wrong. They see that their family member has changed and are aware when there is tension in the home. They nee . . . d information and explanations to help them understand what is happening. Children often imagine things that are worse than reality.

Parents, older siblings and other family members can help dispel fears and anxieties. Help your child to be supportive of their family member by talking to them about mental illness. Be honest but optimistic.

Talk to your child using language and explanations that are appropriate to their age level and maturity (see 'age-appropriate explanations' box on the next page). Look for books and handouts that are written for children. Movies sometimes offer examples that can be used to help children understand. For example, in The Lion King, Simba suffers from depression after the death of his father, Mufasa. Simba's appearance, loss of energy, and lack of interest as he slowly proceeds through the desert provide a concrete example for children to visualize.

Comparing mental illness to other physical illnesses can help normalize the illness. If they have some knowledge of another chronic illness such as asthma, you can use it as an example to help children understand that ongoing care is needed and that people have re-occurrences of symptoms.

It is important to be educated about the particular disorder you're dealing with. If your child asks you a question you don't know how to answer, be honest and tell them you don't know. Let them know you will try to find out.

If a child has seen violent or suicidal behaviour, situations requiring police intervention or any other traumatic incident, don't underestimate how terrifying the experience can be. Help your child to express their feelings.

What you say and do regarding your family member's illness will probably influence your child more than anything you tell them to do.

Suggestions for What to Talk About

Ask your child what they think is the reason for why their family member has been acting differently. Use their response as a way to begin talking about mental illness. Children, especially young children, often believe that if something happens in their world, it is linked to something they did. Ask your child if they somehow feel they are to blame for their family member becoming ill. Reassure your child that their family member's mental illness was not their fault. Mental illness is nobody's fault.

Explain that mental illness can make a person act in strange, confusing or sometimes scary ways. Using alcohol or street drugs can make people do things they would not normally do. Ask your child about the way their family member acts and how it makes them feel. Help your child to express their feelings. Let them know that feelings are neither right nor wrong. It's okay and natural for them to have the feelings they're having.

Here are some other suggestions:

- Reassure your child that adults in the family and other people, such as doctors, are trying to help their family member get better.
- Make sure your child knows what to do and who to call if they don't feel safe.
- Explain to your child that many people still don't understand what mental illness is—an illness of the brain. The brain is an organ of the body just like the heart, liver and kidneys. Sometimes it can get sick, just like other organs.
- Help your child to realize that when they try to talk about their family member's illness, their friends (and even adults) may make fun of it. They may say things that aren't true or they may not know what to say. Practice with your child what they might say to their friends and other people.

- If your child witnesses your family member being taken to hospital involuntarily, help them to understand what happened and why it happened. For example, "Your brother suffers from an illness that prevented him from knowing what was best for him. Just like you have had to do things you didn't want to but we knew were good for you. Sometimes when a person is ill, other people need to decide what is best for them."
- Always remember to let your child know that you are there to listen if they do want to talk.

Here are some questions children commonly ask:

- Why is my [family member] acting this way?
- Is it my fault?
- Can I catch it?
- Will they always be this way?
- Do they still love me?
- Why it this happening to our family?
- Who will take care of me if my mom/dad gets sick?

Age-appropriate Explanations

Toddlers and preschool children can understand short, simple sentences that provide concrete information. For example, "Do you remember when you had [cold, chicken pox, measles]? You didn't feel like doing anything and you were sometimes grouchy. It wasn't because you didn't love us or wanted to be that way, but because you didn't feel good. Mommy sometimes doesn't feel well right now and she needs to sleep to help her get better. She still loves you and me, but she can't show it right now." Or "When Daddy is sick, he has difficulty going to work." Abandonment is a major childhood fear, so children need frequent reassurance they will be cared for no matter what happens.

School-aged children can understand more information. They can likely understand the concept of various disorders (e.g., depression, anxiety), but may be overwhelmed by details about medications and other types of treatment. For example, "You know how parts of our bodies get sick sometimes, like when you get a stomach ache or a sore throat. Sometimes a person's brain can get very sick and the sickness can cause a person to feel badly inside. It also makes a person's thoughts get all jumbled and mixed up, so they can't think clearly. These illnesses have names, such as [schizophrenia]."

Teenagers have the ability to understand more complex explanations about mental illness and how it is treated. They are better able to express their own thoughts and feelings. Concerns they may have include: "Will I inherit this illness?" or "What will others think?" (stigma).

Important Messages Children Need to Hear

- Mental illness is a medical illness
- With treatment and support, their family member will get better

- They did not cause this illness to happen
- They cannot make the illness better
- Illnesses affect the way a person thinks, feels and behaves
- Reminders that it is the illness speaking, not their parent, when they say hurtful or frightening things

Adapted from Helping Children Cope, Mood Disorders Society of Canada

(2) SORROWING

The five stages of grief:

- **Denial:** "This can't be happening to me."
- **Anger:** *"Why is* this happening? Who is to blame?"
- **Bargaining:** "Make this not happen, and in return I will _____."
- **Depression:** "I'm too sad to do anything."
- **Acceptance:** "I'm at peace with what happened."

YOU ARE SORROWING : the LOSS of a loved ones health is such a shock

While loss affects people in different ways, many people experience the following symptoms when they're grieving. Just remember that almost anything that you experience in the early stages of grief is normal—including feeling like you're going crazy, feeling like you're in a bad dream, or questioning your religious beliefs.

Shock and disbelief—Right after a loss, it can be hard to accept what happened. You may feel numb, have trouble believing that the loss really happened, or even deny the truth. If someone you love has died, you may keep expecting them to show up, even though you know they're gone.

Sadness—Profound sadness is probably the most universally experienced symptom of grief. You may have feelings of emptiness, despair, yearning, or deep loneliness. You may also cry a lot or feel emotionally unstable.

Guilt—You may regret or feel guilty about things you did or didn't say or do. You may also feel guilty about certain feelings (e.g. feeling relieved when the person died after a long, difficult illness). After a death, you may even feel guilty for not doing something to prevent the death, even if there was nothing more you could have done.

Anger—Even if the loss was nobody's fault, you may feel angry and resentful. If you lost a loved one, you may be angry at yourself, God, the doctors, or even the person who died for abandoning you. You may feel the need to blame someone for the injustice that was done to you.

Fear—A significant loss can trigger a host of worries and fears. You may feel anxious, helpless, or insecure. You may even have panic attacks. The death of a loved one can trigger fears about your own mortality, of facing life without that person, or the responsibilities you now face alone.

Physical symptoms—We often think of grief as a strictly emotional process, but grief often involves physical problems, including fatigue, nausea, lowered immunity, weight loss or weight gain, aches and pains, and insomnia.

Coping with grief and loss tip 1: Get support

The single most important factor in healing from loss is having the support of other people. Even if you aren't comfortable talking about your feelings under normal circumstances, it's important to express them when you're grieving. Sharing your loss makes the burden of grief easier to carry. Wherever the support comes from, accept it and do not grieve alone. Connecting to others will help you heal.

Finding support after a loss
Turn to friends and family members—Now is the time to lean on the people who care about you, even if you take pride in being strong and self-sufficient. Draw loved ones close, rather than avoiding them, and accept the assistance that's offered. Oftentimes, people want to help but don't know how, so tell them what you need—whether it's a shoulder to cry on or help with funeral arrangements.

Draw comfort from your faith—If you follow a religious tradition, embrace the comfort its mourning rituals can provide. Spiritual activities that are meaningful to you—such as praying, meditating, or going to church—can offer solace. If you're questioning your faith in the wake of the loss, talk to a clergy member or others in your religious community.

Join a support group—Grief can feel very lonely, even when you have loved ones around. Sharing your sorrow with others who have experienced similar losses can help. To find a bereavement support group in your area, contact local hospitals, hospices, funeral homes, and counseling centers.

Talk to a therapist or grief counselor—If your grief feels like too much to bear, call a mental health professional with experience in grief counseling. An experienced therapist can help you work through intense emotions and overcome obstacles to your grieving.

Coping with grief and loss tip 2: Take care of yourself

Need More Help?
Helpguide's Bring Your Life into Balance mindfulness toolkit can help.

Face your feelings. You can try to suppress your grief, but you can't avoid it forever. In order to heal, you have to acknowledge the pain. Trying to avoid feelings of sadness and loss only prolongs the grieving process. Unresolved grief can also lead to complications such as depression, anxiety, substance abuse, and health problems.

Express your feelings in a tangible or creative way. Write about your loss in a journal. If you've lost a loved one, write a letter saying the things you never got to say; make a scrapbook or photo album celebrating the person's life; or get involved in a cause or organization that was important to him or her.

Look after your physical health. The mind and body are connected. When you feel good physically, you'll also feel better emotionally. Combat stress and fatigue by getting enough sleep, eating right, and exercising. Don't use alcohol or drugs to numb the pain of grief or lift your mood artificially.

Don't let anyone tell you how to feel, and don't tell yourself how to feel either. Your grief is your own, and no one else can tell you when it's time to "move on" or "get over it." Let yourself feel whatever you feel without embarrassment or judgment. It's okay to be angry, to yell at the heavens, to cry or not to cry. It's also okay to laugh, to find moments of joy, and to let go when you're ready.

Plan ahead for grief "triggers." Anniversaries, holidays, and milestones can reawaken memories and feelings. Be prepared for an emotional wallop, and know that it's completely normal. If you're sharing a holiday or lifecycle event with other relatives, talk to them ahead of time about their expectations and agree on strategies to honor the person you loved.

When grief doesn't go away

It's normal to feel sad, numb, or angry following a loss. But as time passes, these emotions should become less intense as you accept the loss and start to move forward. If you aren't feeling better over time, or your grief is getting worse, it may be a sign that your grief has developed into a more serious problem, such as complicated grief or major depression.

Complicated grief

The sadness of losing someone you love never goes away completely, but it shouldn't remain center stage. If the pain of the loss is so constant and severe that it keeps you from resuming your life, you may be suffering from a condition known as complicated grief. Complicated grief is like being stuck in an intense state of mourning. You may have trouble accepting the death long after it has occurred or be so preoccupied with the person who died that it disrupts your daily routine and undermines your other relationships.

Symptoms of complicated grief include:
Intense longing and yearning for the deceased
Intrusive thoughts or images of your loved one
Denial of the death or sense of disbelief
Imagining that your loved one is alive
Searching for the person in familiar places
Avoiding things that remind you of your loved one
Extreme anger or bitterness over the loss
Feeling that life is empty or meaningless
The difference between grief and depression

Distinguishing between grief and clinical depression isn't always easy, since they share many symptoms. However, there are ways to tell the difference. Remember, grief can be a roller coaster. It involves a wide variety of emotions and a mix of good and bad days. Even when you're in the middle of the grieving process, you will have moments of pleasure or happiness. With depression, on the other hand, the feelings of emptiness and despair are constant.

Other symptoms that suggest depression, not just grief:

Intense, pervasive sense of guilt.

Thoughts of suicide or a preoccupation with dying.

Feelings of hopelessness or worthlessness.

Slow speech and body movements

Inability to function at work, home, and/or school.

Seeing or hearing things that aren't there.

Can antidepressants help grief?

As a general rule, normal grief does not warrant the use of antidepressants. While medication may relieve some of the symptoms of grief, it cannot treat the cause, which is the loss itself. Furthermore, by numbing the pain that must be worked through eventually, antidepressants delay the mourning process.

When to seek professional help for grief

If you recognize any of the above symptoms of complicated grief or clinical depression, talk to a mental health professional right away. Left untreated, complicated grief and depression can lead to significant emotional damage, life-threatening health problems, and even suicide. But treatment can help you get better.

Contact a grief counselor or professional therapist if you:

Feel like life isn't worth living

Wish you had died with your loved one

Blame yourself for the loss or for failing to prevent it

Feel numb and disconnected from others for more than a few weeks

Are having difficulty trusting others since your loss

Are unable to perform your normal daily activities

REMEMBER:

When you're grieving, it's more important than ever to take care of yourself. The stress of a major loss can quickly deplete your energy and emotional reserves. Looking after your physical and emotional needs will help you get through this difficult time.

Title:
Death's Like A Mystery
WORDS TO THE FIRST SONG I RECEIVED IN 1975
Julie Ann Geddes

DEATH'S LIKE A MYSTERY
IT IS A SPECIAL GIFT
THAST OUR LORD GIVES TO US
THERE IS A GLORIOUS PLACE WHERE WE ONCE ABIDED
WITH OUR GOD—

CAN THIS BE ASKS MY SOUL
ARE WE CHILDREN OF GOD
DO WE TRULY HAVE A PLACE WHERE WE'LL RETURN

I CAN'T REMEMBER ANYTHING OUT THERE
THAT IS BEYOND THE VEIL
OUR SAVIOR MADE IT CLEAR
OUR FAITH WOULD OPEN UP HIS TRUTHS

KEEP YOUR FAITH AND YOUR HOPE
AND LET CHARITY YOUR GUIDE
DO THIS AND YOU'LL TRULY FIND
YOUR WAY BACK HOME
by *Julie Geddes*

MEET ON THE SHORE

there'll come a day—when we meet on the SHORE

there will no more sorrow be—

We wil be near our Loved Ones Dear—

LET US PRAISE OUR LORD

SO, everyday we must have faith in our LORD

Hold on to the Iron Rod and Pray

ENDURE TO THE END

(3) SUFFERING

THE PATH OF HEALING

There is a Truth that applies to everyone and it is that we all need healing and growth in some area. Yet, we all need assistance.

WE ALL WANT TO BE HEARD RIGHT?
THERE IS A LAW THAT WORKS AND NEEDS TO BE TRIED
AND IT IS WHEN WE GIVE SOMETHING EVEN THE VERY THING
WE MAY LACK AND CRAVE THAT IS WHEN IT IS RETURNED TO US TEN FOLD.

The College of Mental Health Counseling at www.collegemhc. com provides this summary of the
The following is based on the text "Effective Counseling Skills: the practical wording of therapeutic statements and processes" by Daniel Keeran, MSW, found at http://www.amazon. com/Effective-Counseling-Skills-therapeutic-statements/ dp/1442177993

The College of Mental Health urges the public to learn counseling skills to prevent an alleviate depression, anxiety, family breakdown, addiction, suicide and other mental illness and distress

The path of healing focuses on putting thoughts and emotions into words in order to be supported and validated or normalized.

With the help of a counsellor, self-awareness leads to self-acceptance which leads to power and mastery over the trauma.

EMOTIONAL TRAUMA TO THE PRESENT

1. Identify the emotion in the current reaction by saying, "What emotion came up in the recent situation? Fear, anger, guilt, sadness, some other feeling?"
2. Explore the recent reaction by saying, "Describe what was happening when you had that feeling? What words would you use to describe what pushed your buttons?"
3. Using the person's own words describing what triggered his reaction, say, "If you were to review your life from early days to the present, what's another time you experienced something similar?" (Use the person's descriptive phrase or word instead of 'something similar'.)

The last step above will take the person to the source of pain or trauma . . .

These healing steps need to be repeated as long as it takes for the person to report feeling better.

1. Invite the person to talk about what happened, by saying, "Talk about what happened back then."
2. Invite the person to identify and verbalize the range of painful emotions associated with the event, by saying: "What emotions come up inside as you talk about that? Is it a little fear, anger, guilt, sadness, or some other feeling?"
3. Help the person process the process, by saying, "What's it like talking about this so far?" or "Is it OK to talk about this?"
4. Validate the emotions, by saying, "It makes sense, it's normal that you feel that. It fits what you have been through. Anyone would feel the same who went through that."
5. Help the person understand the affects of the event on his life now, by saying, "What are some ways that experience and the emotions have affected your life and relationships now?. Validate how the person has coped with the traumatic event and the affects on his life, by saying, "It makes sense you would have done that because you are trying your best to survive the pain of what happened."
7. Help the person visualize how their life can be better, by saying, "How do you want your life to be different if you had power to make it better? Describe the life you want."

8. Reinforce the feeling of hope, by saying, "What are the possibilities of what you can do?"

9. Validate steps the person has already taken, by saying, "You have already taken forward steps in your healing. It's not easy to let go. It takes courage to face the pain and move through it to a new life."

For more information see http://www.ctihalifax.com
Daniel Keeran, MSW

SETTING HEALTHY BOUNDARIES

- When you identify the need to set a boundary, do it clearly, without anger, in as few words as possible. Do not justify, apologize for, or rationalize the boundary you are setting. Do not argue! Just set the boundary calmly, firmly, clearly, and respectfully.

- You can't set a boundary and take care of someone else's feelings at the same time. You are not responsible for the other person's reaction to the boundary you are setting. You are only responsible for communicating the boundary in a respectful manner. If others get upset with you, that is their problem. If they no longer want your friendship, then you are probably better off without them. You do not need "friends" who disrespect your boundaries.

- At first, you will probably feel selfish, guilty, or embarrassed when you set a boundary. Do it anyway, and tell yourself you have a right to take care of yourself. Setting boundaries takes practice and determination.

- When you feel anger or resentment, or find yourself whining or complaining, you probably need to set a boundary. Listen to yourself, then determine what you need to do or say. When you are confident you can set healthy boundaries with others, you will have less need to put up walls.

- When you set boundaries, you might be tested, especially by those accustomed to controlling you, abusing you, or manipulating you. Plan on it, expect it, but be firm. Remember, your behavior must match the boundaries you are setting. You can not establish a clear boundary successfully if you send a mixed message by apologizing for doing so.

- Most people are willing to respect your boundaries, but some are not. Be prepared to be firm about your boundaries when they are not being respected. If necessary, put up a wall by ending the relationship. In extreme cases, you might have to involve the police or judicial system by sending a no-contact letter or obtaining a restraining order.

- Learning to set healthy boundaries takes time. You will set boundaries when you are ready. It's your growth in your own time frame, not what someone else tells you.

- Develop a support system of people who respect your right to set boundaries. Eliminate toxic persons from your life—those who want to manipulate you, abuse you, and control you.

Daniel Keeran, MSW

MY COMMENT: In times of suffering it seems our defense mechanisms will come forth and measure what we can and cannot handle at that time and block much—later on when its our own idea we will want to tell our story as much as possible and try to make sense of it all. There is no need to force anyone to tell or remember all the details. If and when the person needs to bring this forth it will be of their own choice and timing. It is very important when they do share their story to give as much support as possible and be sensative to how much they are affected by sharing. Be sure to titrate the session to what they can handle.

Another thing to do is to make all your statements about yourself QUESTIONS instead of final statements. This will help so you are not feeding the alarm system in brain.

By: Julie Ann Geddes
I wrote a song when struggling with my Challenges be cause the music I receive helps me Fly Above my trials.

WORDS BY MARNIE HAZE BURNS my daughter
Theres a little girl, inside her heart
she's lost and hurt . . . she's in the dark.
Yes it's over now, it's over.
Theres a tiny soul still tyring to be
the little girl she could'nt see.
. . . and she still remembers.
Please let this flower bloom,
I wish I could have helped her,

what was she like, i tried to know.
I cant imagine what she hoped for.
Her little hands, her teary eyes,
did she beleive the wicked lies.
Please let her go.
She wanted love she could'nt find.
She could'nt trust she couldnt hide.
A million stars in the sky tonight,
She would have wished a million times.
The morning may have brought her peace,
or that special dolly she came to need.
The puzzle peices just never fit there in her life
and as the trail of helplessness subsides
theres a light.
She will forever look back, its better this way
its over now, its over.
Delicate is she today, she's given all her strength away
and has made the world a better place.

(4) STRUGGLING

WITH GETTING INTO PHYSICAL SHAPE

Two things you need to do consistently each day.

ONE: Keep an eating journal:
Write down honestly all you eat for the day:

Breakfast, Lunch, Supper and snacks
If it was too much—write down what you need to follow.
You will gain control by keeping track daily of eating.

TWO: Do legs lifts five to six days a week
This is a total body workout—lay on your side lift your leg up and down as far as you can—work your way up to 50 or 100 times on each leg.

If you do this consistently you will get quick results.

Word of Wisdom: Stay aways from too much of anything. Foods or substances that you know are not good for you.

MY COMMENT: STRUGGLING WITH RELATIONSHIPS
Whatever our struggle in a relationship is we will benefit by applying these few quick references into our daily lives . . . as we try to maintain our relationships.

CONTRACT IDEA: This can work in many different situations as a couple or family/ group. REMEMBER IT TAKES TWO.
We all have strengths and weaknesses so its never just one person causing the problems. If you want to have a great relationship with someone study the Virtues. The onenvirtue that is most essential in a relationship is "Consideration" for each other. So, find someone who gives you the same consideration that you give them.

Simply Make a "CONTRACT" ONE thing you want the other to change; they have to also try to change one thing you want them to change. So, the relationship can grow. Its usually the same thing over and over that blocks relationships. If one is not doing their part/contract then the other one does not have to either. It can only be one thing at a time.

This does not always work the first trys but one must remember that it will take a few trys and to never give up. POST THIS ON THE FRIDGE ; ALONG WITH THE SIGNED CONTRACT

~ this will take a few times to get the hang of it. Each time one of you fails the other is off the hook does not have to keep their promise. But, if you want it to succeed the key is to agree to start over and support one another and give each other time to work on this one promise. Its important to keep working on the contract you made with one another.

~Struggling with addiction: reach out for support
The solution to this problem may not be that hard, you just need to find out why do you feel down when you are alone. If the reason was unsolved problems then at least start to take actions or if the reason was lack of self confidence then start to build your confidence. Whatever the cause is just find it then try to take action towards removing it rather than escaping to a temporary addiction that will solve nothing.

ANGER: Struggling with anger?
Take responsibility for the anger you exhibit ; its your actions. There is no place for blame.

1. Take responsibility and power: accept that anger is a choice of when, how, and if to express it or not. Make a commitment to avoid using anger to control, intimidate, or punish others.

2. Unresolved anger from past abuse can be therapeutically vented in a safe counseling setting using methods such as role play or an empty chair.

3. The healthy expression of anger in a relationship can be achieved with a single non-judgmental assertive statement: "I feel angry when you (describe the observable behavior of the other), because (describe the observable affect on one's life)." Example:

   "I feel angry when you don't call to let me know you will be late, because then I can't plan my evening." The passive person who is afraid of raising issues at all, can leave out the feeling word or perhaps substitute a soft emotion (e.g. sadness or fear) for the word angry.

4. Do not vent anger toward others or accuse others, e.g. avoid "You" statements such as "You always . . " or "You never . . "

5. Understand that there is always a story behind others' behavior and remain open to understanding the story so that the angry person does not have to rely on anger to make his point.

6. For offering criticism or negative feedback, try asking permission to do so.

7. Always avoid physical violence (hitting, throwing, slamming), blaming, judgmental terms, name-calling, threats, yelling, and sarcastic tone and put-downs.

8. Focus on current issues and avoid bringing up the past as people often disagree on memories of what happened. Agree to disagree on the past and then bring the discussion back to the present issue.

9. In receiving anger, avoid reacting and use a soft voice tone and sincerely reflect the angry statement so that the angry person feels understood.

10. Remember that the person who is angry with you, is also angry with others and perhaps toward himself. View the angry person as hurt, wounded, and powerless by resorting to anger.

11. The ability to hear and respond to angry criticism requires inner strength to set one's own needs and feelings aside.

12. Before asserting your own view, use the sincere reflective statement to convey understanding of the angry person's point of view. Example: "So you feel angry when I don't call to let you know I will be late, because then you can't plan your evening. Is that what you are saying?"

13. Anger may be a familiar habitual default reaction in which reason and power to choose are by-passed. Be determined to change the default reaction.

14. Anger toward others may also reflect uncaring negative self-talk that can be recognized and transformed into positive, supportive, caring, encouraging, reassuring self-talk that one needed to hear from healthy parents. See the paper on "Counseling for Depression and Anxiety" on academia.edu.

15. Anger may be an unhealthy way of hanging on to the struggle with uncaring parents reoccurring in the present relationship. Anger hangs on to the old struggle. To help the person let go of the struggle, help him become aware

of the soft vulnerable feelings such as fear and sadness that are often beneath the anger.

16. Anger may be an unhealthy way of making contact or of being close to others because healthy caring closeness is too frightening or unfamiliar.

17. Help the angry person move to the feeling under the anger by saying things like, "What feeling is under the anger? Sadness, fear, guilt, some other feeling?"

18. Soft feelings often communicate to others more easily than the hard feeling of anger. Example: "I feel sad and afraid when you . . "

19. To reach beneath the anger, say, "If you were to let go of the struggle, what would you have left?" The person answers, "Nothing." Then say, "What feeling comes up inside when you think there is nothing left?" The person answers, "Sadness."

    This awareness can help the person let go of the struggle.

20. The passive person is often afraid of expressing anger outwardly because of the need to protect themselves or others from a feared outcome. Help the passive client process anger by using other words such as frustrated, annoyed, perturbed, and cheated.

21. Give the passive person the assignment to try the assertive statement—directed in role play, then directed toward the counselor, then directed with permission to someone in his life with a report back on what happened. Congratulate the person for his courage and success.

22. Move beyond power and control by problem solving issues and reaching agreements with timelines to implement any agreement. See the paper on "Making Peace in Groups and Relationships" on academia.edu

23. Avoid trying to settle difficult or conflict-related issues when driving, going to bed, waking up, eating, rushed, in public, or during activities for relaxation, e.g. taking a walk. Be sure the setting is safe and private.

24. Generally avoid interrupting a person who is venting angry feelings, and when possible use a sincere soft voice tone and reflect the angry person's point of view to help him feel understood.

25. When you or the other person is feeling too angry to talk reasonably, say, "I'm not able to talk right now, but I do want to talk about this as soon as possible."

26. If the other person is withdrawn in angry silence, invite him periodically by saying, "I'm ready to talk now if you want to."

27. While anger may be expressed aggressively, passively, or assertively, the healthiest expression is usually assertive. The ultimate goal is to learn how to express or withhold anger intentionally in a way that has the most effective, healing, and healthy outcome. Assess the safety and risk. Avoid expressing anger toward a policeman or an abusive spouse or perhaps an employer.

Daniel Keeran, MSW

Struggling with Depression/Anxiety

Daniel Keeran, MSW, has been a professional counselor and therapist for over 30 years. He has provided counseling and training to thousands of professionals and the public through his private practice, seminars, and training courses.

Depression can be caused by chemical changes in the body, physical illness, and different types of loss. Very often, depression and anxiety are the result of self-defeating life patterns forming unhealthy neural pathways that can be healed by incorporating caring self-talk and by supporting self-worth and assertiveness. We tend to do to ourselves and to others that which was done to us in childhood. Now as adults we must give to ourselves all the healthy things we needed from healthy parents. Here are some things to do to change the inner-dialogue foundations of depression and anxiety:

Step 1. Write down the negative things you think about yourself, others, and your circumstances.
This activity will bring to your conscious awareness the negative thinking and self-talk that is common to many kinds of depression and anxiety. The negative and self-critical self-talk demoralizes the ego and manifests as feeling down, blue, sad, anxious, fearful and self-doubting. This low mood and anxiety then affect sleeping, eating, and low energy. Common examples of negative self-talk are: I am incapable, I can't do it, I am unlovable, I am a failure, I failed again, I can't do it, No one wants to talk to me, No one cares about me, etc.

Step 2. Write down statements that are self-caring, nurturing, reassuring, supportive, and validating.

This exercise helps to identify the opposites of the negative self-talk: I can do it, I have strengths and abilities, I am caring and kind, I can get what I need and want, I deserve to be happy, I can succeed, I am just as important and valuable as anyone else, My pain is normal for what I have been through, etc.

Step 3. Write down negative things parents said or communicated to you when you were growing up.

Here you can write down what you thought parents felt about you by what they said or did such as: I wish you were never born, I do not like you, I do not care about you, I care about alcohol more than I care about you, I do not want to be around you, You are in the way, You are a bother, You should be seen but not heard, You can't do that, You could have done better, You will never amount to anything, Don't cry, etc.

Step 4. Write down things you needed or wanted parents to say to you as a child.

Here you can write the things you wanted or needed parents to say or do such as: I love you no matter what happens, I am so glad you are in my life, You can succeed, It's OK to cry when you're hurt, Everything will be OK, I felt the same as you sometimes, Imagine the possibilities. You are good at that, You are so helpful, You are so kind and caring, etc.

Step 5. Write down what you would do or say if you saw another child being treated the way you were treated in #3.

If you heard someone say mean things to a child or slap a child, what would you say? Maybe you would say things like: You have no right to say that, Be nice to the child, The child needs your love, You need to support your child and be reassuring and caring and loving and affectionate, You need to be encouraging, etc.

Step 6. If you had all the positive things as a child that you needed from healthy parents, how do you imagine your life might be different today?

If your parents had said encouraging, caring, and supportive things to you as a child, how do you imagine your life might be different today? This step helps you formulate and create a vision for how your life can be different in a healthy way. Depression that comes from negative self-talk is a form of self-abandonment and self-abuse. The ultimate self-abuse and self-abandonment is self-harm and suicidal thinking. Conversely, hope, optimism, self-worth, and self-confidence form the basis of a stable mood and sense of security, safety, confidence, well-being, inner peace, personal power, and happiness.

Step 7. Now you must be for yourself all the things that you needed your parents to be for you: encouraging, nurturing, loving, caring, supportive, and reassuring.

This means you need to say to yourself and be for yourself all the positive things you needed from healthy parents. If no one else can give you the caring that you need, who does that leave? Ultimately, you are the one who must care for you. So this means you must choose healthy people to be in your life, and you must be supportive of yourself and of that other healthy caring person you have chosen to be in your life. In this way you will be caring of yourself. Another important piece is to stand up for yourself and support yourself when you are treated badly by others.

Step 8. You must be assertive.
Stand up for yourself by saying things like: I don't like your tone, I deserve more respect than that, I deserve a raise in salary, I feel annoyed when . . ., etc. Take care of that little boy or girl who was abused and mistreated. That little boy or girl is still inside you and needs your protection. Be for yourself now what you needed then as a child. Will you stand up for him or her? When will you start?

The reader can acquire in-depth understanding and healing of childhood experiences affecting adult life and relationships, through a professional and confidential online course by the author at the College of Mental Health Counseling.Daniel Keeran, MSW

Post-traumaticstressdisorder:A   commonanxietydisorder that develops after exposure to a terrifying event or ordeal in which grave physical harm occurred or was threatened. Family members of victims also can develop the disorder. PTSD can occur in people of any age, including children and adolescents. More than twice as many women as men experience PTSD following exposure to trauma.Depression, alcohol or other substance abuse, or other anxiety disorders frequently co-occur with PTSD.

The diagnosis of PTSD requires that one or more symptoms from each of the following categories be present for at least a month and that symptom or symptoms must seriously interfere with leading a normal life:

- Reliving the event through upsetting thoughts,nightmares or flashbacks, or having very strong mental and physical reactions if something reminds the person of the event.
- Avoiding activities, thoughts, feelings or conversations that remind the person of the event; feeling numb to one's surroundings; or being unable to remember details of the event.
- Having a loss of interest in important activities, feeling all alone, being unable to have normal emotions or feeling that there is nothing to look forward to in the future may also be experienced.
- Feeling that one can never relax and must be on guard all the time to protect oneself, trouble sleeping, feeling irritable, overreacting when startled, angry outbursts or trouble concentrating.

Traumatic events that may trigger post-traumatic stress disorder (PTSD) include violent personal assaults, natural or human-caused disasters, accidents, or military combat. Among those who may experience PTSD are troops who served in the Vietnam and Gulf Wars; rescue workers involved in the aftermath of disasters like the terrorist attacks on New York City and Washington, D.C.; survivors of the Oklahoma City bombing; survivors of accidents, rape, physical and sexual abuse, and other crimes; immigrants fleeing violence in their countries; survivors of the 1994 California earthquake, the 1997 North and South Dakota floods, and hurricanes Hugo and Andrew; and people who witness traumatic events.

Many people with PTSD repeatedly re-experience the ordeal in the form of flashback episodes, memories, nightmares, or frightening thoughts, especially when they are exposed to events or objects reminiscent of the trauma. Anniversaries of the event can also trigger symptoms. People with PTSD also experience emotional numbness and sleep disturbances, depression, anxiety, and irritability or outbursts of anger. Feelings of intense guilt are also common. Most people with PTSD try to avoid any reminders or thoughts of the ordeal. PTSD is diagnosed when symptoms last more than 1 month.

Treatment may be through cognitive-behavioral therapy, group therapy, and/or exposure therapy, in which the person gradually and repeatedly re-lives the frightening experience under controlled conditions to help him or her work through the trauma. Several types of medication, particularly the selective serotonin reuptake inhibitors (SSRIs) and other antidepressants, can also help relieve the symptoms of PTSD.

Giving people an opportunity to talk about their experiences very soon after a catastrophic event may reduce some of the symptoms of PTSD.

(5) STARVING

MY COMMENT:

Many people are starving for food in the world.

We must find out the temporal conditions of those we

SERVE. Helping to make others self-sufficient is the goal.

(6) SINNING

MY COMMENT:
The main wisdom I use as a person and Professional Counsellor is to remember that what is considered a sin can be different according to individuals moral code.

I have come to the conclusion that much hate in this world and destruction has been due to people "NOT" SHARING

CHRISTIANITY.
Sharing Christianity is not just sharing what you think it is. Its acknowledging others who profess to be Christians and respecting them. Truly sharing.

Jesus told us in his Sermon on the Mount that we should not judge one another in the least. Why, because of the vital importance of AGENCY.

To be tempted is NOT A SIN (even Jesus was tempted in all things) but we are accountable if we dwell or act on it.

Personal
When I was praying this morning—as usual in the library I had a prompting to share something with you—its how I have learned to apply what I know in my life more so than ever—because when temptations come promising to bring relief—its only temporary relief and makes us feel worse.

- I will apply the LOVE OF GOD in my life. Each morning I will let his love surround me. It will distill on me like the dews of heaven and I will not need to look elsewhere—for this is enough. The Everlasting True Love that created us. by Julie Geddes 2012

Remember God has a Perfect Plan of Salvation.

Six Steps of Repentance:

1. **Feel Godly Sorrow**

   "For I will declare mine iniquity; I will be sorry for my sin." (Psalms 38:18)

   - The first step of repentance is to recognize that you've committed a sin against God's commandments.
   - Feel true sorrow for what you've done and for disobeying Heavenly Father.
   - Feel sorrow for any pain you may have caused toward other people.

2. **Confess to God**

   "By this ye may know if a man repenteth of his sins—behold, he will confess them and forsake them." (D&C 58:43)

   - Pray to Heavenly Father and be honest with him.
   - Tell him of your sin(s).
   - If necessary confess your sins to your local bishop.

3. Ask for Forgiveness

"And it came to pass that I did frankly forgive them all that they had done, and I did exhort them that they would pray unto the Lord their God for forgiveness." (1 Nephi 7:21)

- Pray to God for his forgiveness.
- Forgive others who have hurt you.
- Forgive yourself and know that God loves you, even though you've sinned.

4. Rectify Problems Caused by the Sin(s)

"And if it be stolen from him, he shall make restitution unto the owner thereof." (Exodus 22:12)

- Make restitution by fixing any problems caused by your sin.
- Problems caused by sin include physical, mental, emotional, and spiritual damage.
- If you can't rectify the problem sincerely ask forgiveness of those wronged and try to find another way to show your change of heart.

5. Forsake Sin

"He that covereth his sins shall not prosper: but whoso confesseth and forsaketh them shall have mercy." (Proverbs 28:13)

- Make a promise to yourself and to God that you will never repeat the sin.
- Recommit yourself to obeying God's commandments.
- Continue to repent if you sin again.

6. Receive Forgiveness

"Behold, he who has repented of his sins, the same is forgiven, and I, the Lord, remember them no more." (D&C 58:42)

- The Lord will forgive you when you truly repent with a sincere heart.
- Allow his forgiveness to come upon you.
- When you feel at peace with yourself you can know you are forgiven.
- Don't hold onto your sin and the sorrow you've felt. Let it go by truly forgiving yourself, just as the Lord has forgiven you.

(7) SEARCHING

MY COMMENT:
Along the Path of Life we are all searching for different thigns at different times in our Life-Span. What is it you are searching for?

Support can be given for those searching for careers, work for income and to give referrals and knowledge as needed.

NEVER ASSUME ANYTHING and this is part of being a non-judgmental person.

AGAIN we are instructed to respect others self-efficacy by finding out where they are in life and their successes listening carefully before we give counsel.

I believe in the innate wisdom of every individual. As a counsellor and friend I strive to create a safe environment to explore life issues, while maintaining the belief that each and every person is inherently the expert of their own life.

A SPECIAL GIFT FOR YOU
What . . . is this Faith Hope & Charity?
A special gift . . . that we can use . . . in this world . . . where we live . . .

Open up your mind and your heart . . . to LOVE . . . you"ll see then . . .
when you truly ASK SEEK and KNOCK . . . you will find . . . there . . . you'll find . . .

HONEST ANSWERS ALWAYS . . . IN YOUR HONEST PRAYERS

. . . . and lift your love for God . . . you'll see then yes you WILL see then the HONEST TRUTHS TO KNOW . . .
YES YOU'LL KNOW THEN

by: Julie Ann Geddes

HOW TO DEAL WITH SOMEONE WHO MAY FEEL

(8) SUICIDAL

Just as CPR has been promoted to save lives, it is vital that the general public knows how to assess and prevent suicide. Here are the steps:

1. Notice if the person appears disheveled or the gaze is downward or the voice tone is flat or says things like, "Life's not worth living," or "I hate my life," etc.
2. Ask: "How would you rate your mood right now on a scale of zero to ten with zero meaning life's not worth living and ten meaning life is great?"
3. If the person rates the mood as 5 or under, ask: "Have you had any thoughts of suicide or of harming yourself?" *
4. If the person indicate yes, go to the next step. If the person says, "I don't know," hear this as a "yes" to the question in #3.
5. Ask: "Have you thought about how you might end your life?" If the person says yes, the risk is increased.
6. Ask: "What have you thought about as how you might do it?" If the means is ineffective or non-lethal, such as cutting wrists, risk is lower. If the means is lethal such as using a gun or jumping from a bridge, etc., risk is higher.
7. Regardless of the means, ask: "Can we agree together that if you have thoughts of killing yourself, you will

speak to me personally (not my voice mail) before carrying out a plan to harm yourself?"

8. If the person says "no" or "I don't know," to the question in #7, say: "What I am hearing is that you are in a lot of pain right now and thinking of ending your life, so I am wanting you to go to the emergency room right now and get some help to feel better right away. Will you go? I will make sure you get there safely. Is there a family member or someone I can call to go with you?" Or tell the person you will go with them yourself.

9. Arrange for the person to be accompanied to the emergency room, and call ahead to tell emergency staff you are coming.

10. If the person refuses, then ask the person to wait there with someone while you call police in another room to report that the person has threatened suicide with lethal means. Ask the police to come and accompany the person to the emergency room.

*Note: If the person rates the mood as high (over 6) after feeling consistently depressed, and s/he now reports life is great and s/he is smiling, the risk may be increased because s/he has decided to end their life and have made all arrangements.

Daniel Keeran, MSW

loved one's suicide can trigger intense emotions. For example:

(7) Shock. Disbelief and emotional numbness may set in. You may think that your loved one's suicide couldn't possibly be real.

(8) Anger. You may be angry with your loved one for abandoning you or leaving you with a legacy of grief — or angry with yourself or others for missing clues about suicidal intentions.

(9) Guilt. You may replay "what if" and "if only" scenarios in your mind, blaming yourself for your loved one's death.

(10) Despair. You may be gripped by sadness, depression and a sense of defeat or hopelessness. You may have a physical collapse or even consider suicide yourself.

You may continue to experience intense reactions during the weeks and months after your loved one's suicide — including nightmares, flashbacks, difficulty concentrating, social withdrawal and loss of interest in usual activities — especially if you witnessed or discovered the suicide.

Adopt healthy coping strategies

The aftermath of a loved one's suicide can be physically and emotionally exhausting. As you work through your grief, be careful to protect your own well-being.

- **Keep in touch.** Reach out to family, friends and spiritual leaders for comfort, understanding and healing. Surround yourself with people who are willing to listen when you need to talk, as well as those who will simply offer a shoulder to lean on when you'd rather be silent.

- **Grieve in your own way.** Do what's right for you, not necessarily someone else. If you find it too painful to visit your loved one's gravesite or share the details of your loved one's death, wait until you're ready.

- **Be prepared for painful reminders.** Anniversaries, holidays and other special occasions can be painful reminders of your loved one's suicide. Don't chide yourself for being sad or mournful. Instead, consider changing or suspending family traditions that are too painful to continue.

- **Don't rush yourself.** Losing someone to suicide is a tremendous blow, and healing must occur at its own pace. Don't be hurried by anyone else's expectations that it's been "long enough."

- **Expect setbacks.** Some days will be better than others, even years after the suicide — and that's OK. Healing doesn't often happen in a straight line.

- **Consider a support group for families affected by suicide.** Sharing your story with others who are experiencing the same type of grief may help you find a sense of purpose or strength.

- **Actively grieve and mourn.** Grief is an inner sense of loss, sadness and emptiness. Mourning is how you express those feelings. You might plan a funeral or memorial service, wear black, and carry a somber demeanor. Both grief and mourning are natural and necessary parts of the healing process after a loss.

- **Acknowledge your pain.** If you don't face your grief, your wounds might never quite go away. Accept that the pain you're feeling is part of dealing with grief and moving toward a state of healing and acceptance.
- **Look to loved ones and others for support.** Spending some time alone is fine, but isolation isn't a healthy way to deal with grief. A friend, a confidant, a spiritual leader — all can help you along the journey of healing. Allow loved ones and other close contacts to share in your sorrow or simply be there when you cry.
- **Don't make major decisions while grieving.** Grief clouds the ability to make sound decisions. If possible, postpone big decisions — such as moving, taking a new job or making major financial changes. If you must make decisions right away, seek the input or guidance of trusted loved ones or other close contacts.
- **Take care of yourself.** Grief consumes a significant amount of energy. Your will to live and ability to follow normal routines might quickly erode. To combat these problems, try to get adequate sleep, eat a healthy diet and include physical activity in your daily routine. Consider a medical checkup to make sure your grief isn't adversely affecting your health — especially if you have any existing health conditions.
- **Remember that time helps, but it might not cure.** Time has the ability to make that acute, searing pain of loss less intense and to make your red-hot emotions

less painful — but your feelings of loss and emptiness might never completely go away. Accepting and embracing your new "normal" might help you reconcile your losses.

- Losing a loved one is devastating. Someday, however, the sun will shine again. The day will seem brighter and your life will go on — even if it'll never be quite the same.

GUILT—IF ONLY I'D DONE SOMETHING MORE

Perhaps the most intense anger you experience will be the way you feel about yourself. This anger is closely linked with feelings of guilt. "But I just talked with him!" "Why didn't I listen?" "If only . . . I should have . . ." etc. You'll think of a lot of others.

If the deceased was someone with whom you had regular close contact, your guilt possibly will be intense. And if the death came as a complete surprise, you will be desperately searching for reasons. A person who completes suicide has usually given out some clues, and as you look back on the last few months (or years) maybe you can now see some hints you missed earlier. You'll wish you'd recognised the problem early enough to do something about it.

Perhaps you were aware of the deceased's suicidal feelings and you did try to help. You may have thought you had because in the time proceeding the death you noticed he or she seemed to be feeling a lot better and you relaxed your concern. You need to know it's not uncommon for a suicidal person to feel better once the decision to die has been made. The problem has not been resolved, but the victim has found an answer—suicide.

As you are trying to cope with your guilt feelings, try not to criticise yourself too harshly for your behaviour toward the victim while he was alive. Are you now wishing you could have found the right solutions or offered more support? Thoughts like "I shouldn't have gone to the movie", or "I should have been there", may constantly be running through your head. If you had stayed home, or if you had been with him, the suicide could and possibly would have happened at another time. If you feel your presence at a particular time could have prevented the suicide, you are assuming too much. Of course we all like to think we can help our troubled friends and families, and we do try. But, the person determined to complete suicide is likely to accomplish it.

If you realistically feel there was something you could have done, face it, think about it, and accept it. Your loved one can't be helped any more, and you need to go on with your life. You can learn from, and grow with, your experience.

Some people believe an individual has a right to end his life. The term 'rational suicide' is used to describe a suicide that has been thought about, and planned, perhaps as a way of dealing with a painful terminal illness. This is an area of controversy, and whether you accept it or not, what you do need to think about is that the suicide was an individual decision—rational or not.

It was his choice, not yours. You may accept this intellectually long before your emotions accept it.

What value does your anger or guilt have in the healing process and beyond? Rather than letting the hurt isolate you, share your time and understanding with someone else who is hurting. You can provide friendship and support. Get involved with others; actively support suicide prevention services in your area, or any worthwhile cause or issue that means something to you.

(9) SAD

MY COMMENT: ALL of the "S" Words are a result of some kind of LOSS along our path of life. Sadness is the result of LOSS. Being able to share your story is such a support in such times. Tears are healing. Do not be too quick to stop the emotions.

Just one person that you can talk to and feel listened to with confidential unconditional regard.
IS SO VALUABLE
Sometimes we all feel like this turtle . . . life is going slow and nowhere and we feel like everyone is watching and quacking at us. Unconditional positive regard, a term popularly believed to have been coined by the humanist Carl Rogers . . . is basic acceptance and support of a person regardless of what the person says or does. Rogers believes that unconditional positive regard is essential to healthy development. People who have not experienced it may come to see themselves in the negative ways that others have made them feel. By providing unconditional positive regard, humanist therapists seek to help their clients accept and take responsibility for themselves. Humanist psychologists believe that by showing the client unconditional positive regard and acceptance, the therapist is providing the best possible conditions for personal growth to the client.

I believe in the innate wisdom of every individual. As a counsellor I strive to create a safe environment to explore life issues, while maintaining the belief that each and every person is inherently the expert of their own life.

(10) SCARED

MY COMMENT:

Being scared at the appropriate time is when we are in danger. IF the feeling lingers and re-occurs without cause we will need to overcome this strong alarm system in our brain.

I learned a simple trick to use in times of panic . . .

Our internal alarm system is wired such that it can only respond to the words it hears us think or say. We ourselves no matter what we do cannot turn off our panic attack—the alarm system in our alone can turn the off button. So, in this case when we are starting a panic attack/ being scared for a real reason or not . . . we must consider what we say and think. Since the alarm system has turned itself on . . . we would like it off before it escalates. When we think words such that beg it to get worse . . . the alarm system is thinking oh there must not be cause for alarm . . . after hearing that repeatedly the alarm system turns itself off. I have practised this in my life consistently and it will work. (Julie Geddes)

I wrote this song in 2008—Julie Geddes
PEACE BE STILL
Are you lonely
Did it go bad?
Is there no where to turn?

Just let your heart hear the voice within you . . .

Know that your never alone and listen . . .

To the Still Small
Voice Within You!

And you'll know what I mean
Peace Be Still, He Is Near You . . .

HE WHO CALLS ONE AND ALL!
TO HIS KINGDOM WITH LOVE
LET YOUR BROKEN HEART
BRING FORTH
FAITH . . .
SO YOU'LL FOLLOW THE LORD!

REMEMBER: God's Word is the only thing that can chase away our doubts and fear this is a powerful statement it is something that literally works not only in doctorine but as we actively use it in our thoughts.
-Isaiah 26:3
To ward off fear from worldly disharmony or discord. VOCALLY CALL UPON GODS WORDS ~ WHEN TIMES ARE DARKEST ~

The Lord has said to us: 'Therefore, fear not, little flock; do good; let earth and hell combine against you, for if ye are built upon my rock, they cannot prevail' (D&C 6:34, 36). We must fortify ourselves. That sure spiritual fortification is found in two words—Jesus Christ."

King James Version (KJV) PSALMS 1:33

But whoso hearkeneth unto me shall dwell safely, and shall be quiet from fear of evil.

"When through fiery trials thy pathway shall lie,

My grace, all sufficient, shall be thy supply.

The flame shall not hurt thee; I only design

Thy dross to consume and thy gold to refine."

(11) STRESSED

Managing Stress Steps? Here They Are:
MIND YOUR WORDs
KEEP SMILING
RECOGNIZE YOUR VICTORIEs
JUST EAT THE RIGHT FOODs
MOVE

The best effect of the 5 SIMPLE STEPS MANAGING STRESS STRATEGY is that it dramatically increases your chances to easily get into the state of coherence.

To be in the state of coherence means being able to find the perfect balance where the resistence of your body to any external or internal force is minimal. This immediately brings you to the conclusion that the state of coherence is the best power saving mode. The mode which helps you relax and restore in the most efficient way!

This is a key step in order to overcome stress because to fight it we need to be strong. It is as simple as this—we need power.

You just need enough personal strength to communicate effectively, to add value in what you do, to identify your enemies, to foresee their actions, to be at the right place at the right moment . . .

The 5 SIMPLE STEPS MANAGING STRESS STRATEGY gives you the steps, which if followed will make you stronger and stronger and eventually will let you overcome stress.

- The first step toward change is to become more aware of the problem. You probably don't realize how often you say negative things in your head, or how much it affects your experience. The following strategies can help you become more conscious of your internal dialogue and its content.
- **Journal Writing:** Whether you carry a journal around with you and jot down negative comments when you think them, write a general summary of your thoughts at the end of the day, or just start writing about your feelings on a certain topic and later go back to analyze it for content, journaling can be an effective tool for examining your inner process
- **Thought-Stopping:** As you notice yourself saying something negative in your mind, you can stop your thought mid-stream my saying to yourself "Stop". Saying this aloud will be more powerful, and having to say it aloud will make you more aware of how many times you are stopping negative thoughts, and where.
- **Rubber-Band Snap:** Another therapeutic trick is to walk around with a rubber band around your wrist; as you notice negative self-talk, pull the band away from your skin and let it snap back. It'll hurt a little, and serve as a slightly negative consequence that will both make you more aware of your thoughts, and help to stop them! (Or,

if you don't want to subject yourself to walking around with a rubber band on your wrist, you'll be even more careful to limit the negative thoughts!)

Replace Negative Statements:
A good way to stop a bad habit is to replace it with something better. Once you're aware of your internal dialogue, here are some ways to change it:

- **Milder Wording:** Have you ever been to a hospital and noticed how the nurses talk about 'discomfort' instead of 'pain'? This is generally done because 'pain' is a much more powerful word, and discussing your 'pain' level can actually make your experience of it more intense than if you're discussing your 'discomfort' level. You can try this strategy in your daily life. In your self-talk, turning more powerful negative words to more neutral ones can actually help neutralize your experience. Instead of using words like 'hate' and 'angry' (as in, "I *hate*traffic! It makes me so *angry*!"), you can use words like 'don't like' and 'annoyed' ("I don't like traffic; it makes me annoyed," sounds much milder, doesn't it?)

- **Change Negative to Neutral or Positive:** As you find yourself mentally complaining about something, rethink your assumptions. Are you assuming something is a negative event when it isn't, necessarily? (For example, having your plans cancelled at the last minute can be seen as a negative, but what you do with your newly-freed schedule can be what you make of it.) The next time you find yourself stressing about something or deciding you're not up to a challenge, stop and rethink, and see if you can come up with a neutral or positive replacement.

- **Change Self-Limiting Statements to Questions:** Self-limiting statements like "I can't handle this!" or "This is impossible!" are particularly damaging because they increase your stress in a given situation *and* they stop you from searching for solutions. The next time you find yourself thinking something that limits the possibilities of a given situation, turn it into a question. Doesn't *"How can I handle this?"* or *"How is this possible?"*

(12) SERVING"

MY COMMENT: EXPERIENCING THE "S" WORDS IN LIFE—ENABLE EACH ONE OF US TO BETTER SERVE OTHERS—WHO ARE GOING THROUGH THOSE SAME THINGS.

When we serve its not only the one being served that benefits but also who serves.

". . . but behold I say unto you, that by small and simple things are great things brought to pass."—Alma 37:6

I don't know all the reasons the Lord tries us in this life, I think he wants to know whom he can trust. The Lord found he could trust Abraham because he was willing to offer his own son as a sacrifice if that was what the Lord wanted.

B. INTERSTICIAL CYSTITIS BY THOSE WHO KNOW

I asked friends affected by IC—some men as well as many women if there was one thing they would like the WORLD TO KNOW about Intersticial Cystitis what would it be?

THEY ALL AGREED: the fact that
I.C. Oftentimes IS severely painful and debilitating

Many also stated: They always feel so sad because they cannot be what they want to with and for the people they love.

JULIE KINDT GEDDES
MY URINARY BLADDER REMOVAL—August 2010
I do not want to get into my story details but will answer a few questions my friends asked me from the I.C. Support Group I found only after my bladder removal surgery. Which I continue to support.I will always be part of the I.C. Family.

I had Intersticial Cystitis for 25 years myself. I was diagnosed by my Urologist in 1990. So I know about this Chronic Disease first hand. Intersticial Cystitis began mildly for me—when young and slowly degenerated through the years.I am surprised to find many young people with the disease already progressed to severe end stages of bladder functioning and disabilitating symptoms.

What brought me to the decision of bladder removal?

It was progressively degenerating and disabling. An easy choice.
This question was the most common one that I was asked after my surgery.Well, I was around 45 and knowing how this disease was progressing for the worse—I asked my Urologist about the possibility of bladder removal. He told me yes that could be in my future but he would prefer I wait until I am in my 50's because it is disfiguring for younger women and can cause self-esteem problems. Also, if they were taking out all of the bladders at request there would be an overload of surgeries going on at any given time I suppose. So, that gave me hope for in the future if I needed it removed. Several years passed and my bladder degenerated further.None of the treatments that use to give a little relief for a short time were working anymore. I was grateful for my Urologist approving a disability application when I could not work anymore in 2002.Even though it is not much. I would also suggest taking a witness to your

appointments who can testify to your specialist how much you are suffering and disabled.

What was the worst part of bladder removal?

Well, the worst part was the anticipation of having pain after the surgery as I recovered.I was not looking forward to that.

I was very very scared when I was waiting to go in the operating room for fear of waking up in severe unbearable pain. This was my ONLY concern. I had great faith in the doctors capabilities and skills and trust in God. I was blessed in this worry because when I went in the operating room they put a spinal line drip into my back to give me direct pain medications and anesthesia.

Due to the fact I cannot take the narcotic Morphine.So, when I woke I had no pain just tenderness. After four days of no pain . . . at which point it would have had time to heal some resulting in less pain. They removed the spinal line in my back. It was a bit of a struggle after that recovering with the pain that came but I know I was spared the worst part and am ever grateful for that blessing.

Also, the Urologists reported that my small bowel the short part they removed to use for my Urinary Stoma actually died immediately upon them cutting it out to use. It went very gray.

They told me that never happens. They did not know what to do at first and were very concerned. The Urologists decided to go ahead and sew it in finish the surgery and *pray for the best. The next day circulation started returning to the stoma what a relief.*

~BLESSING~

How long was recovery?

This is a great question because we know its different for everyone.
Each of the seven days in the hospital there was a complication which they would say if its still there tomorrow we will treat it.
Each time the next day I was healed.

How am I now one year later from removal of urinary bladder?

Pain free—would be the way I would express how I am doing!
I am better than ever. It took about a year to truly be able to do any type of physical activity full out without feeling a bit of tenderness but its perfectly normal now. I am ever grateful to my Urologist whom did my operation very successfully.
I believe the removal of the whole bladder is necessary to be free from the IC.

How did your husband and children deal with your chronic Disease?

That is a question many asked me.

They can best explain it themselves thus I am including in this book to share some of their thoughts in poetry.

At first they had to be convinced and accept the problem but after they became more aware they would do whatever necessary.

I tried to be a good example. First being patient with those around us! I was not the only one experiencing the LOSS of my health.

It took time for the reality to sink in that I was not getting better.

I still suffer immune system problems that are disabling.

PSALMS 16:11—Path of Life
I FEEL THE TOUCH OF THE MASTER'S HAND
UPON MY HEAD OFTEN
It is through (acting) not being acted upon = AGENCY
Exercising faith in the word of god in my life and
the Gift of the Holy Ghost.
That my burdens are light and healing has come many times.
Not only for my physical health but also mental health.

My Patriartical Blessing I received as a Valiant Member of the Church of Jesus Christ of Latter-day Saints has been a sweet guide. I was adjured to develop my talent to Love My Fellowmen. That many would come lean on me for my kindly care, advice, guidance and support along the Path of Life. I would be a friend to all who come. Along with many other things I was told I would have sweet dreams of the Lord's own promptings and that he would always be by my side as I listen to the still small voice that shall come to me as I lay half-awake, half-asleep.

I have had visions and the Holy Ghost preparing me much ahead of time for many things in life.

My Relationship with our Redeemer Jesus Christ started as a child for me as I listened to the word of God in Sunday School Lessons and has continued even throughout my life.

By: *JULIE GEDDES*

What IC Teaches Me IC= INTERSTICIAL CYSTITIS
.by Jaime Coronado Aragon
I wondered what this time of pain for me was teaching them.
I hope that because of this disease IC they learn compassion.
I hope they learn to nurture and protect
I hope they see how much they impact others
I hope they learn courage to face their fears
I hope they see my gratitude when they help me into bed
I hope they learn that they can depend on each other in hard times
I hope they find peace in the simple things and cherish every day
I hope they learn laughter and love are the best medicine
I hope they learn that illness doesn't equate to weakness
I hope they learn to have Faith in God.
I hope they learn to have patience with themselves and others
I hope they know I love them even when mommy can't play
They blessed me with their smiles and told me they would take care of me today. Lesson indeed.
I hope that from my beautiful children I learn humility

I hope that I learn to be more loving and more positive

I hope that I learn to forgive myself of my limitations

I hope that I learn its ok to ask for help and to accept it with gratitude, not attitude

I hope that I learn to show gratitude better

I hope that I learn that Im a power unto my self and to never let IC dictate who I am

I hope that I learn that though others won't understand my pain, I can be understanding of them

I hope I can learn to stop worrying about those who dont care

I know that I am watched over by my Heavenly Father

I know that I am blessed to have a man who loves me

I know that I have incredible children and they are my teachers

I know that I am lucky to have friends who love me

I know that this disease IS real

I know that even in the darkest night, longest day, loneliest moment, there are others like me who reach out

I know that someday this fire of pain will refine me into the strongest of steel

I know that when I walk, I DO NOT walk alone.

I'm still ME

By Billy M. Aragon (companion of someone with I.C.)

For those who don't know me, you may think I'm weak, but to my family & friends, I'm very unique.

I'm strong & courageous, and full of love to give, and though outgoing, you can't see for a hard life I live.

I have Interstitial Cystitis, "IC" for short, an incurable disease, that's tearing me apart.

It affects my social life, my love life and all,

And physically ruins me, on my knees I crawl.

A pain like no other, people don't understand,

Though it affects hundreds, not only women, even a man.

Even children have this, yet no one knows why,

There just isn't any answers, no matter how we try.

Socially its hard, to have any true friends,

Though I have some, a true hand they wont lend.

And to be in love is rough, nobody wants a "disabled" partner,

The don't want the hassle of living any harder.

And physically.. well I'll put it like this,

Since my disease, my whole life I've missed.

When people run.. I walk, when the laugh.. I want to cry,

The pain gets unbearable, so much I'd rather die.

People say get up your "fine", why do you lay in bed,

Try exercising a lil, walking or do anything instead.

They say its all mental, its all in my mind,

I wouldn't let it get to me they say, if the disease were mine.

Well regardless of what people say, this sickness is hard,

I have it, its got me till death do us part.

I'm limited to what I can do, I wish I could be happy just like you,

And though it's a lil harder, I try to do everything that you do.

So if you ever meet someone who has "IC"

Forget what people may say, remember I'm still "ME"

SANDRA JON MAXWELL

I was only 24 years old when I was initially diagnosed with IC, I had just recently given birth to my second son, I am now 40 years old and have had IC for a very long time now, I feel very blessed to have been able to have my boys before getting this disease, I feel that having IC has made stop and realize that life is not a race, and the perfect house means a lot less now than perfect health, I do feel that women today feel they have to" be everything" and" do everything" in order to succeed, now that my boys are teenagers I have the insight that I did not have before, before I had IC I never asked for help, I could never say "no" to anyone this disease had made me put myself first now for the first time..I am grateful everyday for my family and for Jesus Christ and all he did for us and to show us how to be a better person, I know that my body is not perfect anymore but I know with faith in Jesus Christ one day I will be free of pain, I now dont take much for granted like I use to, I look at other people even strangers and when our eyes meet I smile, being in chronic pain has made me feel so much closer to the spirit world something I never experienced before, I do feel closer to God and I know it is because of this disease, but I love God and my family enough to fight another day and that is all that matters . . .

Sandra Jon Maxwell
Shirley Wade Has IC

My name is Shirley and I have IC. My journey actually begin in the late 1980's when I was about 40. At that time I had a UTI which wouldn't go away. My family doctor referred me to a Urologist. After seeing him, he said I didn't have an infection and suggested that I have a cystoscopy. He told me I had an inflamed area in my bladder and he cauterized it! I now know this was be beginning of IC and that the area should not have been cauterized. He never mentioned Interstitial Cystitis or gave me any reason for the inflammation. After having that procedure I did have relief and I was blessed that the IC basically went into remission.

I started having problems again in June 2010 when I thought I might be getting a Urinary Tract Infection and was put on antibiotics. I took the medication and was drinking cranberry juice and getting worse. I didn't realize that the acid in the cranberry juice was causing me more pain! I returned to the doctor and a urine test indicated no infection. The doctor said I was having bladder spasms and prescribed Ditropan. I was told to stop drinking soft drinks, eliminate caffeine, chocolate, artificial sweeteners and MSG. I did that and did get some relief then started to have increased pain and spasms. By September I was having increased pain, pressure and spasms so I went back to the doctor and got another prescription for Ditropan. He referred to a GYN who did a pelvic exam. He thought hormone pills would help my bladder and pelvic pain. After a little over a week on hormones and the Ditropan, I was so sick that I had to stop taking the hormones and the Ditropan. I decided it was time to go to a urologist. I had read about IC on the internet and from what I read I was afraid I had Interstitial Cystitis. The urologist found blood in my urine and advised that I needed to get tests to check for cancer and IC. I had a cystoscopy with hydro distention and was diagnosed with IC. Two weeks later I found out my biopsy was fine but I still had IC. The doctor put me on Elmiron (the only medication actually prescribed for IC) and Atarax. Most doctors also prescribe a low dose of the anti-depressant Eavil to help with the pain. In my case, I am already on an anti-depressant so it wasn't prescribed at that time. I was feeling better for a week or so until 2 weeks before Christmas. I started having really bad pelvic pain with shooting pains and cramps. I had increased low back pain and even my inter-thighs hurt. I could barely walk because of the pain. I returned to the doctor and was started on a bladder cocktail regime (once a week for 9 weeks). That is when a catheter is inserted and medication instilled into the bladder for relief. The cocktails did seem to help until my ninth one. Later I tried the cocktails again but they caused increased pain so I had to discontinue them.

While I consider myself blessed that the medical community's awareness of the disease is better than it was a few years ago, there is still a long way to go and more research needs to be done to find a cause and a cure. Most people have never heard of Interstitial Cystitis Syndrome it is a very painful bladder condition. It impacts every aspect of your life and affects those around you. There are different treatments that are used to try to give relief but sadly what works for some IC sufferers doesn't work for others. It is really an ordeal. Most of what IC sufferers learn is from their own experiences and those of others who have IC. When you first find out you have IC, you are afraid and feel helpless because you know there is no cure.

Most doctors do not want to prescribe pain medication which I cannot understand. I would not want to take pain medication if I didn't need it! The pain and discomfort is hard to deal with. A lot of IC sufferers have 'IC belly' where the lower belly is extended to the point that you look 4 to 6 months pregnant. Your entire tummy from your navel down is sore and very uncomfortable. Wearing loose fitting clothing is necessary to avoid a painful IC flare. Diet is an very important part of the treatment for IC. Even driving or riding in a car or other mode of transportation can trigger a painful IC flare from the vehicle's motion.

I tried to deal with the pain without pain medications but my pain got so severe I had no other option. My Primary Care Physician did try to help me by adding Eavil 10 mg twice a day and Ultram. That helped at first but I needed something stronger so she prescribed 2 Lortabs a day and I tried to take gabapentin which is for nerve pain. I was unable to take the gabapentin due to unbearable side effects. I have just recently had to start seeing a Pain Management Specialist. The journey is a hard one and I am still searching for the right combination of treatments to give me some of my life back. I miss the joy in my life and pray with God's love and help and the love of my husband, family and friends, I will find that much needed relief.

All my prayers are with my fellow IC sufferers. Anyone who doesn't have IC can't understand how it affects your life. God Bless!!! Please help us by praying for a cure and spreading the word about IC!!!

Emily C. Muir Redd—IC STORY

I cannot even remember how many doctors I saw over a period of three years trying to get help for the pain I felt and endured day after day. I remember eating at an Asian restaurant for a friends birthday and after the meal the pain and urgency came on so fast and so strong that I could barely make it to the car. I thought I must have a UTI and called the doctor the next morning. Once again I was told it was not a bladder infection. I became frantic to figure out what was wrong with me and did days, weeks and maybe even months of research. Finally, one night I was lead to a web page, it was a page I had been on several times before but this time I saw something about a disease called IC. I went on to read about the disease and discovered I had every symptom. After years of seeing countless doctors I had finally found my answer and pretty much diagnosed myself, I was confident I had interstitial cystitis. My pain was so severe that luckily my aunt had a friend that was a urologist and he got me into surgery that very week to diagnose whether or not I had the disease.

The doctor performed a cystoscopy and hydro-distention of the bladder. I have never in my life experienced such horrific pain as the pain I had when I woke up from that surgery. I woke up literally screaming out for somebody to help me. I was still groggy but had to be carried to a toilet where I could not move but just sat crying and crying from the bladder pain and urgency. Once I was able to finally see the doctor he confirmed what I already knew to be true. During the procedure my bladder could not hold the water. My bladder walls began to rupture and hemmhorage uncontrollably. It was so sever the doctor had to discontinue the procedure. I had a horrible and severe case of I.C. The next four years of my life were hell!

Being properly diagnosed with Interstitial Cystitis did not solve my problems like I thought a proper diagnosis would. It only made things harder, and more frustrating. My urologist told me that I.C. was such a horrible disease that my husband would probably leave me, I would never be able to hold down a job and I would have a miserable life. He told me he was just trying to be up front and honest with me. Hence, I left that urologist and am still searching for one that can properly help me today.

I continued to see countless doctors and even traveled to California and Denver to meet with "so called" specialists to seek help for my daily misery. I finally decided to go to a local pain clinic in Salt Lake City. There I found the most compassionate and understanding doctors I had met with thus far in my journey. They knew more about I.C. than any urologist, OB, or other doctor I had seen over the years. I had tried just about every I.C. medication and procedure, including Elmiron, bladder installations, trigger point injections and even physical therapy. I had also tried every herbal remedy I heard of or read about. I went on the I.C. diet and avoided anything acidic. Nothing helped.

I finally met with a wonderful, compassionate woman who not only had a medical degree but also had a PhD in women's health. She became the answer to years of fervent prayers. We tried new things and some worked and some didn't. Even though I had been seriously sick over the last 7 years I still longed to have another baby. She understood this and together we tried new things and finally she helped me ween off my medications and try something new. It actually worked and for the first time in 7 years I was not totally pain free but my pain levels were so low that on some days I didn't even notice my bladder. My urgency became less and I slowly fell into remission and got pregnant again by IVF. After I was pregnant it helped me to establish total remission. I enjoyed almost an entire year of remission. My baby is almost 9 months old now and I am just starting to feel the signs of the I.C. returning.

Having I.C. is not like being diagnosed with diabetes or even cancer. Those diseases have treatments that can actually help. And although I.C. also has treatments, the treatments don't work for many of us that suffer daily. There is no known cause and no known cure. I.C. is an invisible disease which in my opinion is the absolute worst kind. Not only do we suffer from the physical pain but there is an emotional pain that is extremely and almost impossible to deal with. Nobody understands what it is like to suffer from I.C. unless you have it or have a loved one who has it. After I was properly diagnosed people still thought it was "all in my head." I have never felt so alone. Even my loved ones, close friends and family didn't understand. I was judged for taking pain medication and muscle relaxants. The emotional battle was endless, I did not feel like I was the mother or wife I wanted to be or dreamed I would be. I felt like a burden and a complete failure. My husband has been my rock and my champion. Even though I do not think he fully understand the extent to which I have suffered he has been there in the night to carry my back to bed and help me get my medications or whatever I may need. When my I.C. is at it's worst I'm lucky if I get 3 hours of sleep a night because the urgency can be so extreme.

I hope my story will someday help somebody else know that they are not alone in this fight. When I was first diagnosed there was nothing I wanted more than to talk to somebody else who also had I.C. I wanted to know I was not crazy and this disease really was inside my body. I now know many other women who also suffer from this horrific, painful disease and I know I am not alone. I do not know what the future holds for me but just knowing that I am not alone gives me strength beyond measure. I pray that doctors will start taking this disease more seriously and listen to those who suffer from it. I pray that one day doctors will become more educated about it and of course my ultimate prayer is that there will be a cure. Until then I hope and pray that our voices will be heard.

Emily C. Muir Redd

Salt Lake City, Utah Thank you Julie! I left quite a bit out but Wasn't sure how long you wanted it. I wished I would have included just how scary it can be to leave your house and worried about finding a bathroom especially with kids in tie etc. Oh well, it was therapeutic to write. I pretty much was very emotional as I wrote it. Last night I had a terrible night and I'm frightened for the future. When will your book be out & who is publishing it??

JOI SWEET-HONNIBEE TAYLOR

HERE'S MY STORY: HI MY NAME IS JOI GRAY, AND I'M 15 WITH IC. IC HAS CHANGED MY LIFE, IT'S TURNED IT UP SIDE DOWN. I WENT FROM BEING AND A AND B STUDENT, NOW I HAVE TO GET MY G.E.D BECAUSE OF IC. I WAS NOT ABLE TO MOVE ND GO TO SCHOOL. I'M GOING TO B A PREACHER AS WELL, I'M NOT EVEN ABLE TO GOT TO CHURCH. THE DOCTORS WHERE JUST MEAN AND NASTY. I WAS TRAUMATIZED AND LEFT WITH URETHA SYNDROME, I LEFT THOSE DOCTORS AND ENDED UP AT 1 OF THE BEST SO CALLED DOCTORS OFFICE, VCU. VCU WAS NO BETTER THAN THE FIRST DOCTORS. THEY LIED, THEY GAVE ME SO MUCH HELL WITH GETTING THE ELMIRION. I DIDN'T HAVE TO GET THIS BAD. ALL OF MY REAL SO CALLED FRIENDS I THOUGHT I HAD LEFT ME WHEN IC HIT. I MEAN I DAY I'M PERFECTLY FINE AND THE NEXT I'M HURTING TO BAD TO ME. THESE LAST FOUR YEARS HAVE NOT BEEN GREAT AT ALL. BUT I HAVE A LOVING GOD THAT WAS RIGHT BESIDE ME, HE SAID HE WILL NEVER LEAVE ME NOR FORSAKE ME.

FINALLY I LEFT VCU AND ENDED UP WITH DR. LONNY GREEN, HE'S A GREAT DOCTOR AND HELPS ME WITH EVERYTHING. WHAT VCU TOOK TO DO IN 2YRS(WHICH WAS GIVE ME THE ELMIRION) HE DID IN 1 OFFICE VISIT. I'M HERE TO SAY THAT THERE IS HOPE, I KNOW THERE IS BECAUSE OF LIVING PROOF. THANK GOD. I'M ABLE TO MOVE BETTER AND I DON'T HURT AS MUCH. GOD IS GOOD. I HAVE SO MANY HOPES OF GETTING MY OWN FOUNDATION FOR TEENS DEALING WITH IC. I REALLY HOPE TO GET IT OR BECOME A PART OF ANOTHER FOUNDATION.

Written by Marnie Haze Burns (our daughter)

"take a moment and see
where are we going
we started out so small
we're still growing
now your knowing . . . you've made it some how
but your feet have led you down
ohhhh along the way
along the path of life

take this moment believe
from the inside out
stones and turns have tried you
at times we want out
now its showing . . . you've made it somehow
you've followed close behind him
ohhhhhh along the way
along the path of life

iv found the secret here
iv found it all but one
and looking for the way discovered
the path is narrowed and done
follow his way . . . follow him
in his foot steps walk and live
follow his way . . . as your way
desire will take you . . . walk by faith
ohhhhhh along your way

Amy Fulk, 20, Illinois

As a young lady, I would never have imagined that something like Interstitial Cystitis could drastically changed my life. It's like a bullet that I never saw coming my way, but I'm now thankful that it did.

At 17 years old, a diagnosis that you have never heard of, let alone you can't even pronounce, is a really scary thing. I was diagnosed with IC on March 3, 2010, after having laproscopic surgery. My entire life changed that very day. From there on out, I would have to change my eating habits and my whole lifestyle.

One week before my high school graduation, I signed to play volleyball on a full ride scholarship to a community college in northern Illinois. At the time, I was going through DMSO treatments and putting myself in horrid pain from training so hard each and every day. In the fall of 2010, I started college as a Business major while playing my heart out on the court. All I had ever wanted was to use my athletic abilities to get into college so that my family would not have the heavy burden of paying my costs. Unfortunately, in the middle of our season, I had to make the hardest decision of my life and give up my scholarship, drop out of all my classes, quit my job and I had to move back home, all thanks to IC.

That December, I was transferred on to the doctor who has become my life saver. After five months and many medication and treatment changes, I decided to try the InterStim to help my frequency and urgency. I was given the choice of learning to catherize myself, but I desperately wanted to find another way to help myself. After both surgeries were complete in May, 2011, I was feeling better than ever-I finally felt like I was on the right track to having as close to a normal teenage life as possible!

Even though the InterStim was such a huge success for me, I still had to deal with the ten-level pains on a daily basis. I even lost most of my hair and eyebrows due to medications as well. Life with IC is definitely not easy, but I see it as a sweet sorrow. It's a blessing in disguise to me.

Last summer I enrolled as a college freshman at a different community college as a Pre-Med major. I plan on transferring on to a prestigious medical school to get my doctorate in Urology and specialize in Interstitial Cystitis and other diseases associated with it. It hurts my heart to see so many amazing, beautiful and intelligent people suffering in silence and it is my personal goal to make sure that no one will have to live their life the way that I have had to. Every day is a hard battle for me and even though I'm in twenty-four seven pain, God, my family, and my IC support system will always be there to offer support, encouragement and advice. This disease and all of these people have helped me in so many ways and I owe it all to them to help find a cure for all of us.

MY IC / BLADDER REMOVAL STORY . . . by Ellen Wolfson on Thursday, September 1, 2011 at 11:22am

Ever since I can remember, I have had to urinate often. Even in Kindergarden, my teacher had to call my Mom in to talk to her about the amount of times I asked to go the bathroom! In High School, I made sure I went after every class, So I wouldn't have to ask to go to the bathroom during the next 45 minute class! At 22, it hit me full force. I was working at an accounting firm, and was on my way back down the hall to my office from my 25th bathroom trip of the day, when I suddenly I got the WOSRT stabbing kind of pain in my bladder. It felt like knives were poking at my bladder. I stopped and doubled over. From then on, the pain never went away and the urinating got more and more frequent. I went from Dr. to Dr., Some refusing to even see me.. I didn't know why . . . But only until I was diagnosed with IC did I learn how many Doctors did not want to deal with "IC" patients. With my symptoms, I guess they "prejudged" my condition before even seeing me!! Then there were the other doctors telling me there was nothing wrong without bothering to even do any tests. FINALLY diagnosed by an IC professional Doctor at Cedar Saini, in Beverly Hills. I was relieved to know they had found out what the problem was so I could get treated already, and move on with my life. Little did I know, that day was going to change me, and my life forever. I live in Los Angeles at the time where I was born and raised. I was happy, outgoing, social, hard working, spontaneous, adventurous, I with lots of Great friends, A wonderful boyfriend . . . I loved life! My Dr. did a cysto/hydro and my bladder capacity was down to a TINY 25 cc's (1/4 cup)—My bladder was the size of the walnut!! It was hardened, scared, and ulcerated. The pain was beyond anything I can describe. The first treatment my Doctor started me on DMSO. I'll never forget how bad it burned my bladder-I almost jumped off the table. I went for 2 more and each time it hurt my bladder more and I could not hold the medication in. It seemed to make my bladder feel worse. My Urologist referred to A Top IC Specialist in San Diego @ UCSD. I thought by some hope he could "fix" my bladder. When I finally got to see him, he did another cysto/uro and said my bladder was so bad, that he'd never seen someone so young with a bladder like that. He wanted me to try injection treatment into my bladder, Elmiron, and several other medications. ALL which failed. At this point I was 25. I had decided to leave Los Angeles, it was too stressful, I wanted to be closer to my IC treatments, and in a much more peaceful environment. As we all know STRESS can effect our IC A LOT! I picked up my entire life, left the job that I loved, my friends . . . and to move to San Diego. My quality of life was ZERO. My Boyfriend hung in there with me. My parents retired a year later and moved down to San Diego too, So they were my rock. I went in for a routine appointment on a December day. My Doctor came in, sat down, and told me the words I did NOT want to hear. He told me after not responding to any treatments, the only option was to remove my bladder. Again—Happy because I would be out of pain, but I had no idea what that all entailed, And what it would mean for my future. When he explain the "Indiana Pouch" to me, It sounded Wonderful!! I would not have to wear a bag on the outside, so how bad could it be? He being a specialist, I trusted in him and was so relieved to hear it would finally be OUT! He explained to me that the "Indiana Pouch" is a reconstructed bladder made out of large and small intestines. The only thing was he removed my urethra, so I can't "pee" the normal way.. I have a tiny hole (stoma) on my stomach—just left of my right hip, and every time I have to urinate, I have to use a catheter. It doesn't hurt at all. The only thing is you have to make sure you have a clean catheter everywhere you go or you cant go the bathroom! lol They need to be sterile or you can easily get a UTI or Kidney infection. In my case, I had never had a UTI or Kidney infection before my bladder was removed. Once it was removed, I had so many, My left kidney is now half the size of the right, it's scarred, And I have kidney damage. I had a kidney obstruction a few months after my first surgery. I felt great for about 5 years, I had my life back, no pain, it was amazing. But slowly I started getting the "IC" pain back, urinating more, and eventually started leaking from my stoma (this is all over a 9 year period) To make a long story short, the last 2 years I spent leaking like crazy and no doctor said they could do anything about it, so at night I had to start wearing a bag to keep from making a mess atleast 3 x's a night. Then it got even worse, I started leaking 24/7, So I had to start wearing the bag 24/7. I was depressed, didn't want to leave my house . . . Wearing the bag just caused more and more kidney infections. My Doctor didn't bother to tll me that IC CAN come back in the pouch. So when I started getting all the symptoms back—I was devisted. I started the same treatments ALL over again again with no luck. My capacity shrunk from 1000 cc after my surgery to 187 cc's.. I went from Dr. to Dr. and all of them told me they could not take anymore intestine to enlarge my bladder or I would end up with "the runs" (aka:short gut syndrome) for the rest of my life. My only option was to wear a bag on the outside. I did not want that. By the grace of God, we found a Dr. at UCLA who only deals with female urology who women who have had their bladders removed. Right away the Doctor said "I can fix you". So last Feb.2010, I went thru major surgery, he took more of the small intestine to enlarge my bladder. IT WORKED! NO MORE LEAKING, and My capacity is up to 500 cc's. I did have 2 bowl obstructions after that surgery, and I still suffer pain and flare ups. BUT still . . . I can not complain at all compared to how I was before. I still have IC in my new bladder, I can only hope the capacity stays. I DO still experience pain—Nothing like before when having the bladder but it's there. I get nerve pelvic nerve pain, As my Doctor best describes it "you can remove the bladder, but you cannot remove the nerve endings", I still get "flares" with burning pain, especially around my period. Stress is still a trigger! And I get a STRANGE "Phantom" pain and feel like I have to "urinate" the "normal way" lol It's freaky:) lol One IC sister on. here had her bladder removed by the same Dr. I did, yet she has a bag on the outside. He told her he hasn't done Indiana pouches since mine because the risk of IC coming back is too high. Never in a million years did I think it could come back in intestines!! But the Dr. said it's SOMETIHING in the urine that's attacking. I just wish they would figure this out already. I know the PAIN, Suffering, and HOW MUCH it effects your daily life . . . I feel like I lost the best years of my life. I did. I never married, or had kids because this took over my life and no one wanted to deal with someone in a situation like this. I had no IC friends, no support groups, . . . I felt like a freak. I can't tell you how much meeting all of you my IC SISTERS, has changed my life. I have people who understand and care. I am here for each and everyone of you if you ever have any questions, need a shoulder to cry on, an ear to listen or someone to vent to. HUGS!!!!!

POEM
BY: ANTOINETTE TASSON TELCK

You're there in the morning
You're there in the night
You keep us company
. . . With all your might
Your words and actions
Are as loud as can be
You make them known
With fanfare and glee
You call us friend
And stay by our side
You know all about us
There's nothing to hide
You keep us in sight
You call out our name
You wine us and dine us
And take all the blame
There's never been a friend like you
Who makes us talk and act insane
We can count on you like no other
For you, my friend, are the one called 'PAIN'
Try as we might
To get you to leave
You only squeeze tighter
To us do you cleave
We used to be angry
That you never would go

But now we accept you
And go with the flow
You've changed our life
You've caused us to wake
You've given us cause
For decisions to make
So thank you for coming
And making us see
That hope is alive
And dreams will be
You're helping us travel
On a much different road
You've aligned us with others
Who carry this load
So here's to all
Who know you as well
You've given us purpose
And stories to tell
Our banner is "CURE"
Our disease has a name
INTERSTITIAL CYSTITIS
We are fanning the flame
We won't back down
We won't go away
Until there's a cure
It will happen some day
Our lives will be lived
We won't live in vain
Our lives will have purpose

Even though we have pain
Our legacy is firm
Never give in
Until there's a cure
Until we all win
So up to the roof tops
Out the front door
Tell all our stories
Then tell them some more
Tell them and tell them
Until we are heard
Lift up the banner
"CURE" is the word.

Vicki Naeyaert Julie, I thought of a few things maybe for the book: 1. Advise is don't tell your child to hold their pee or you drank to much water for the day, my mother always did that to me, so she never took me to the doctors cause she felt I drank to much water. My docotr told me if I would have been treated as a kid i might not be this bad. 2. Also I have the interstim and my battery is dead . . . I dont have health insurance now so, always check with the medtronic person and ask them how would they treat this situation if you don't have health insurance later on in life. 3. Always have hope, I used to think I didnt want to live the rest of my life like this then my Uncle comminted murder/suicide for fear of getting divorced, I woke up and realized how many people I would have hurt. And that gave me hope.

My battle with INTERSTICIAL CYSTITIS "NEVER GIVE UP"
By Teresa Linton

In 1992 I was living in a suburb of Washington, D.C. and had been employed as a legal assistant for a Washington law firm for 16 years. I was in my 30s, had an active social life, many friends and for the most part a "great life." In March of that year my life would change and the nightmare began.

I developed what I initially thought to be a routine urinary tract infection. My doctor put me on antibiotics and, after taking them for three weeks with no relief, I knew that something else was wrong. Over the next nine months I saw six different urologists. I was urinating up to 30 times a day, and the pelvic pressure was so horrific I had difficulty walking. I was told that I was "stressed out", just "wanted drugs" and that I was "crazy". One doctor actually told me that I was "in denial that my biological clock was ticking."

I had to take a temporary leave of absence from my job and find out what was wrong with me. I did not sleep because of the chronic pain. My family, who gave me support in the beginning, eventually began to believe the doctors. I went from healthy, hard-working young women to a walking zombie.

Things only got worse. My family encouraged me to to seek psychiatric help. When I refused, my brother-in-law, who was a police officer, and the "quack" doctor I was seeing at the time deemed my problem to be stress related, petitioned for a court order and forced me into a psychiatric facility. I put most of the blame on the inability of the doctors to take me seriously. They were able to convince loved ones that "it was all my in head." The doctors at the facility told me that I had a bladder infection and put me on antiobiotics. I pleaded with them to let me leave the hospital so that I could find a specialist but to no avail. My normal weight of 105 lbs. had dropped as a result of the stress I had been under and, because I had to go to the bathroom constantly, they accused me of being bulimic and locked the door to my bathroom. I could only go a few times a day when a supervisor was present. The lowest point came when a case manager at the facility told my family that they should practice "tough love" with me—a popular term usually reserved for those suffering from addictions, moral dilemmas or criminal behavior. I was not engaging in any of these practices, and I was furious; however, I knew that, if I did not play by their rules, I could end up at the facility for months. I was released after 30 days, but I realied that, unless I could prove what was wrong with me and clear my name, I would have a "stigma" attached to me for the rest of my life.

I found a doctor who specialized in female bladder problems and made an appointment. I told him that "I would not leave his office until he found out what was wrong with me." He put me in the hospital, did a bladder distention and discovered that I had petechial hemorrhages and inflammation in my bladder lining. He made his diagnoses—I had interstitial cystitis ("IC"), a chronic inflammation of the bladder. Due to a defect in the bladder lining, IC renders its victims helpless—going to the bathroom 40 times a day is not unusual, and the pressure and constant pain account for sleepness nights. Althought I was relieved to get a diagnosis, I was upset to learn that the cause of the disease was unknown and that there was no cure. The next step was to try DMSO, an anti-inflammatory liquid poured into the bladder which relieves inflammation. I noticed instant relief. I was able to go back to work and maintain a semblance of a normal life. Unfortunately, my system became immune to the treatments after a year and they ceased to work. The pain was so bad that I begged the doctor to remove my bladder. He stated "you don't meet those requirements—that would be like removing your head because you have a headache." Evidently, the bladder has to be scarred to the point of not functioning at all to do this. This process can take years, and it is the last straw. At this point, I had lost my will to live. I actually thought about ending it all, and I wrote a note to my friends insisting that my bladder be removed and studied so that other victims may be spared the agony. But then I thought "everyone else will win" and I carried on.

My next step was to seek disability. When I applied for social security disability the hearing officer stated that "IC is not a real disease" and denied my application. I had to hire an attorney and two years later I was approved for disability. For the next five years I was bedridden. I rarely left the house, and the only that that kept me going was the knowledge tha the FDA was going to approve a drug called "elmiron" which was specifically for IC patients. In 1998 I began to take the drug; it took nine months to work and I began to get relief. I also combined it with elavil, an old tricyclic antidepressant that, in low doses, is a pain blocker.

I began to feel like my old self. By this time the internet had come along, and I met a number of women and a few men who had been through the same experience that I had. I began to see articles in major magazines talking about the disease. I read that more funds were being allocated to study the disease and that the Social Security Administration had named IC as a "coded" disease, enabling victims to get benefits quicker. It seemed that more people were getting diagnosed and that a new awareness was taking place.

I have been in remission for ten years. The drugs that I take do have side effects—a few of which are dry mouth and lack of energy. However, this is much easier to deal with than the pain of IC. I am trying to come to terms with the way I was treated by the medical profession. Although the pain of IC has been compared to the pain of end-stage cancer, it is hard to convince people of the severity of the disease. I often hear "you look fine, you can't be that sick" or "get over it, you are not going to die." Although I feel well enough to work again, job hunting is not going to be easy with such a gap in my resume. Another hurdle that I will have to overcome is that if I return to work "will the pain return?" The doctors have no answer to this, and I would have to convince the disability board that my pain has returned—I sometimes feel that I am between "a rock and a hard place."

The lack of compassion from doctors, family and peers, combined with the length of time it takes to get a diagnose, leave IC victims drained physically and emotionally. Many victims tend to isolate themselves rather than explain the disease over and over again; thoughts of suicide are common in IC patients.

On a positive note, I have to come to realize what a good life I had before IC and not to take anything for granted. Actually, IC is not that rare—over four million men and women have IC and many more may be misdiagnosed. I have become more politically active and have developed a greater compassion for those who suffer from chronic illnesses. I have also become acquainted with a number of women who suffer from IC through support groups on the internet. I think the great compliment I have ever received was when one woman called me her "guardian angel."

For a long time I was embarrassed to discuss my illness and what I had gone through. I am now proud to share my story with others so that they may find some answers. I pray that a cure will be found, and that no one will have to suffer from this devastating illness.

Thank you for reading my story.

KELSEY MIYAKE-IC STORY My life changed as I knew it in September in 2008, I was diagnosed with IC. I remember shortly after I turned 17 I started having UTI's very frequently and was always up at night going to the bathroom. After I was diagnosed my life had changed in so many ways, and not for the good. I just recently had to drop out of school due to my IC, I missed so much that I couldnt finish. Some days I just want to lie in bed and never wake up, I get very depressed when I get a flare up. I dont go out with friends anymore, I dont take long road trips, I dont live a normal 21 year old life! I know I am missing out on so much because of this disease. It is the worst pain I have ever felt inside and out. I am engaged to a wonderful man he has been with me through all of this. Our sex life has also changed, somedays I am fine and somedays I dont even want to be touched. How awful is that? I worry about having children, I want a baby so bad but this disease makes me scared for my life and the childs well being. I can say for myself and for thousands of men and women out there who have this monster inside of them that we hope for a cure very soon, so we can all live our lives like we were meant to.

Sandra Gadzinski

My name is Sandy Gadzinski, I'm 41 yrs. old & I have been suffering wiith IC for over 20 yrs. I was about 19 when I started experiencing the bad pelvic pain. It would come & go when it first started, but as time passed it became more intense & constant. As a teenager I suffered with many uti's. I started my jouney to find out why I was having such bad pelvic pain when I was 22 yrs old. I was being shuffled from one doctor to another, I guess because they didn't know what was wrong so they would just refer me to yet another doctor. I had two Laporoscopies done by the time I was 28 along with countless other procedures, but the doctor would always tell me they couldn't find anything, with the exception of one. He seen that I had very large veins that were twisting, and bulging so at that time he diagnosed me with Chronic Pelvic Conjestion Syndrome, he also told me I had the bladder the size of a very small childs, but none of us put it together, that could be part of the problem. That doctor wasn't afraid to treat my pain, but then he moved away leaving me back at square one. So I continued to suffer without any help from the medical field. In fact, most of the others treated me as if this was psychological (all in my head). Thier was nothing more frustrating than knowing I had something wrong with my body & it was causing me great deals of pain yet nobody was taking me serious. I felt so hopeless & helpless. Over the years I did contiplate suicide several times due to the pain & it being to much for me to bare. It was extremely hard for me to get up & go to work seeing my job was very demanding physically. I would miss alot of work due to this, up to 60 days a year, but I did have family leave papers in place so I couldn't be fired, thanks to the doctor who diagnosed me with Chronic Pelvic Conjestion Syndrome.

I was finally diagnosed with Interstitial Cystitis in 2003. It was such a relief to know what was causing all the pain, but at the same time it was very scary because their is no cure & there was really no treatments I could do to make it easier on me at that time. All I was told was to do was stop eating alot of trigger foods & stop drinking alcohol, coffee, soda, & even tap water, which I did & it did make a difference. I wasn't curled up in a ball crying on the sofa as much, but the pain was still their & very severe. I have no quality of life. I'm unable to be in a relationship because being intimate just causes the pain to be more intense, I can no longer work & be independent, it has taken my ability to be the parent I once was away, the children have had to learn to do alot of things for themselves, things I should be doing as their parent. This disease has completely changed me as a person & has most definetely changed my life. I have no life, IC has control of each day! This has caused me a great deal of depression. I have to take large amounts of pills everyday to control the disease itself, the anxiety, depression, pain, high blood pressure, & the acid reflux. Besides that, I have to cath myself at home every 12 hrs. to give myself the bladder treatment which consists of more medication & steroids mixed together to form a type of bladder cocktail. I also cath when going to the bathroom to get all the urine out because I push as hard as I can & still the urine won't come out on it's own. This is not an easy life by no means. I begged my urologist to just remove my bladder, but because of my age he is reluctant to do something so invasive. They like to wait til the person is at least 50 yrs. old. Us people whom r suffering with this are without a doubt some of the strongest people you could meet. We know this because of what we each go through on a daily basis. I pray for a cure so future people diagnosed with IC do not have to suffer like most of us have to.

I'm grateful I have a very helpful older son, who does so much to help me & the little ones. He decided to go to the local college for the first two years. Hopefully by then I will have more answers & options of what I can do. Also I'm really lucky to have found my IC support groups when I did. My IC sisters have helped me through many dark days & have also helped me find the right doctors closer to my hometown. Julie you are most definetely one of these people. You have given me alot of inspiration and have helped me personally through alot. Thank you for that & for writing this book spreading awareness about how devestating this disease is on ones life. The medical field, family, friends & the public in general need to know more about this bladder condition. I also think that when a person is diagnosed with this disease, she or he should automatically be deserving of the social security benefits. It is impossible to work with this disease, especially when it gets to the point of where it's constant in the persons life and so very severe. Much Love to my IC family, Thank you & big hugs to you Julie!!! ~Sandy Gadzinski~

Written in April of 2000
By: Marnie our daughter

HOW MUCH PAIN CAN YOU TAKE
I SEE IN YOUR EYES
MORE THAN ENOUGH
. . . WHO CALLS THIS FAIR
YOU LAY AWAKE—HOW DOES IT FEEL?
I KNOW YOU HURT BUT

YOUR STRONGER THAN THAT
YOUR SPIRIT IS REAL . . .
WILL HE EVER TAKE IT BACK?
WILL YOU EVER LIVE IN PEACE
WITH YOUR BODY
BECAUSE YOU DESERVE THAT

YOUR FACE IS MY LIGHT
SPEAKING TO ME KEEPS ME HERE
WHERE WILL YOU BE WHEN YOUR GONE
WHEN WILL WE LAUGH
WHEN WILL I SMILE

I THINK OF YOU KEEPING WATCH AT SUNRISE
AND THERE WHEN DARKNESS FALLS
WITH ALL YOUR LIGHT MOM

I LOVE YOU NOW AND I LOVE YOU FOREVER
NOT TILL YOUR GONE
BUT MORE AS SECONDS TIP TOE BY
EVEN WHEN NOTHING GOES RIGHT
BECAUSE YOUR MORE THAN ANYONE

YOUR STRUGGLE IS NEVER FUN
BUT YOU PULL THROUGHT
EVERY TIME
YOUR STRONGER STILL AND I KNOW I AM RIGHT

YOUR MORE THAN ANYONE COULD ASK FOR

AND JUST WHAT WE ALL NEED
SO DON'T GIVE UP
YOU'LL WIN EITHER WAY

HE LOVES YOU AS WE DO
BUT, DO NOT WANT YOU TO LEAVE
SO STAY
YOUR MORE THAN ANYONE COULD ASK FOR
AND JUST WHAT WE NEED
SO STAY!

I LOVE YOU MOM FOREVER MORE

A POEM FROM MY DAUGHTER

I WANT TO HAVE THE WISDOM ; LIKE YOU HAVE
I KNOW IT WILL COME IN TIME
I WANT THE STRENGTH
. . . SEE IN YOUR EYES
I WANT THAT STRENGTH TO BE MINE
I WANT TO AHVE THE PASSION
LIKE YOU HAVE PASSION
I KNOW I WILL IN TIME
I WANT THE CARING
I SEE IN YOUR EYES
I WANT THAT CARING TO BE MINE

I WANT YOUR COURAGE
I WANT YOUR FAITH

BUT I WANT IT ALL TO BE MINE
I WANT YOUR LIVE
I WANT YOUR ATTENTION
BUT I WANT IT ALL TO BE RIGHT

by Marnie Haze Geddes april 2005
to a mother with a Chronic Disease

TO MY MOTHER JULIE GEDDES from Marnie Haze 2007 mother . . . some might think of this day as the day you were born 53 yrs ago. I think of it as another blessed year that you are alive and i really do think (even with all your health issues) you are one of those people who will live past your 100th birthday. Because the world NEEDS you and i need you. So even though i needed a little reminder of this special day, i will never forget you and am so happy that iv had you and will have you for the rest of your birthdays !!!! xo your daughter

POEM MOTHER'S DAY 1996
By: Marnie our daughter

WHY CAN'T I SHOW MY FEELINGS TO YOU
ALTHOUGH I LOVE YOU SOOO
IF I COULD BE AFFECTIONATE
. . . THEN I THINK YOU'D KNOW

SOMETIMES WE FIGHT AND ARGUE
BUT MAKE UP IN AWHILE
I JUST GIVE APOLOGIES

BUT YOU GIVE ME A SMILE

YOUR VERY UNDERSTANDING
YOU HELP ME NO MATTER WHAT
EVEN IF I TURN FROM YOU
YOUR LOVE WOULD STAY WITHIN

WHEN TIMES ARE HARD
AND PAINFUL
YOU GIVE YOUR LOVE TO ME
BUT MOM I DOOOOO LOVE YOU TOO
ALTHOUGH YOU MAY NOT SEE

I'M THE DAUGHTER
YOUR THE MOM
IM GLAD IT TURNED OUT THAT WAY
WE ARE PART OF A FAMILY
I HOPE THAT WAY WILL STAY!

1996 Marnie

Poem by Marnie 1997 Mother's Day
TITLE: MORE

MORE HELPING ME
MORE LOVING ME
. . . EVERLASTING HOPEFULLY
AND WHAT DO I GIVE YOU
AND HOW DO I HELP YOU
AND WHEN DO I TELL YOU
I AM THINKING ABOUT YOU

MORE OF YOUR SMILING FACE
UNDERSTANDING MY MISTAKES
YOU NEVER MADE ME FEEL UNLOVED

AND WHAT DO I SHARE
BECAUSE I AM NEVER THERE
FOR YOU
I NEVER SHOW YOU
AND I CARE

YOUR ALWAYS THERE WITH OPEN ARMS
YOU ALWAYS HAD THAT MOTHERS CHARM
I AN LOVING EVERY BIT OF YOU
EVEN WHEN I SAY I AM HATING YOU
I AM REALLY RELATING TO MY ENEMIES
THEY GET THE BEST OF ME IN MY TEENS

THEN THERE IS YOU WITH
BEAUTY'S GRAND
HOLDING ONTO GODS HAND
AND THAT IS WHY YOU ARE MY WONDER WOMAN

I TRY TO BE LOVING BECAUSE
I LOVE YOU!

POEM

BEING BRAVE

Why am I feeling the way I do?
Why do I feel like I am dying inside?
Will this feeling I have inside of me ever fade?
Why am I feeling the way I do?Why do I feel like I am dying inside?.
Will this feeling I have inside of me ever fade?
What does my family and friends really think of me?
Have I let them down?
Why does life have to be so hard or hurt so bad?
People tell me I choose to have my life like this.
Why in the world would I "Choose" to live my life like this?
I would much rather be happy instead of unhappy mad or angry!!!
BY: LISA ARTIS

GARNET J. GEDDES

ALONE IN THIS LITTLE HOUSE—January 22nd, 2011

I'm here by myself, but I don't feel alone
This little old shack—I'll always call HOME
The mirrors and windows are talking to me . . .
They're gone—but there here peaceful and free . . .
If I could go back I would in a breath
To a Mom and a Dad, who both gave me their best!
Every inch on the floor, every square on the wall-

I can hear them and smell them and still see it all.

I will telll all my children and—such good children too!

About just where they come from and just who was who!

And someday they'll meet them with me by their side.

We'll relive every moment of the life that slipped by.

Memories on memories on memories

I'll Cherish !

Half my future is my past.

Half my heart is BROKEN!

GJG Garnet James Geddes

MOMMA BEAR & GARN DOG

Proudly to my parents : Gavin Joshua Geddes

So another Christmas apart from my family.
As I age, it becomes more clear to me how important Family really IS.
My two big sisters are off molding their own families; and I am here in Vancouver trying to make ends meet—working on my career.
All I know is, with you raising us the way you have, we will all be fine.
I'm starting to Establish myself out here and I feel things are starting to come around the way I want them.

I want to thank you, Mom and Dad, for raising me the way you have and for the unconditional love and support. Emotionally, Physically and even Financially that you have given me my whole life. I would not be where I am today, if I was raised differently. So this Christmas
I want you to reflect on the success we've all shared together and also, the troubles we've overcome together.

MY HEART AND WILL ARE STRONG BECAUSE OF YOU JULIE AND GARNET GEDDES. I LOVE YOU BOTH AN UNDESCRIBABLE AMOUNT.

MERRY CHRISTMAS 2011

C. PATH OF LIFE JOURNAL

THE UTMOST CHALLENGE IN LIFE IS
"YOU"

To visualize . . . is to create a blueprint in your mind

Its rather ironic how someone who thinks of self as a perfectionist is least likely to become anywhere near perfect because ~
The process of becoming better and progressing towards any form of perfection involves many failures and many less than perfect activities and practises that bring us closer to our goal. A perfectionist cannot bear these steps that must be taken to grow.
Any set backs that are less than perfect bring the perfectionist too low for their ego (pride) and they use a host of excuses to cease trying.

When you use this blessing journal you will not struggle with what others may think about you because you know who you are each day as you use this along the path of life.

I AM A CHILD OF GOD

CREATE BALANCE

Daily Schedule

Write down your short and long term goals here each new year:

MONTHLY GOALS/YR.
MY BLESSING JOURNAL

The Blessing Journal is a record of the things in your life that are positive and important to you. Also a way to re-construct your view of self. We often forget many things;even those that happened last week. We must replace the negative space in our minds with positive thoughts;so there is no room for negative.

Also, as we grow and age things change and we may get stuck in a certain pattern of thinking as to what we think is normal and our expectations in areas of our lives. In order to be happy we need to get over those blocks in thinking and decide for ones self what will make me fullfilled in my life now— starting where you are in the Life-Span.

Do not record the negative things only parts of struggles and how you overcame them but otherwise all the things you are happy about.

I found that I threw away my Journal if I had written things I do not want others to see.

This way you are going to get your self-worth internally not from external input. You have set your expectations for yourself to build on.

Briefly record how challenges were overcome.

Blessings come in all shapes and sizes.

It may be a blessing for some just to wake up in a better mood. Even to not have stepped on a lady bug. To having a heart transplant.

Or Significant events like marriage, baptisms.

YOUR JOURNAL IS ~YOUR TRUTH~create a positive view

THE POWER OF POSITIVE THINKING brings self-esteen . . .
which gives one courage to go out and do things that bring
self esteem

AGE:
PLACE:
MONTH / YEAR:

BLESSING JOURNAL
my heartfelt monthly message:

BLESSED TO:

IT WILL BE ALSO A PERSONAL HISTORY when you start from Birth to 20 and so on . . .
BIRTH TO 20, 20-30, 30-40, 40-50, 50-60, 60-70,70-80 B, 80-90, 90-100.

PROGRESS NOTES

DATE: _____   NAME: _____

GOAL (diagnosis)   Ideas to improve

PROGRESS NOTES

DATE: _____   NAME: _____

GOAL (diagnosis)   Ideas to improve

PROGRESS NOTES

DATE: _____   NAME: _____

GOAL (diagnosis)   Ideas to improve

PROGRESS NOTES

DATE: _____   **NAME:** _____

GOAL (diagnosis)   **Ideas to improve**

PROGRESS NOTES

DATE: _____   NAME: _____

GOAL (diagnosis)   Ideas to improve

PROGRESS NOTES

DATE: _____   NAME: _____

GOAL (diagnosis)   Ideas to improve

PROGRESS NOTES

DATE: _____   NAME: _____

GOAL (diagnosis)   Ideas to improve

PROGRESS NOTES

DATE: _____   NAME: _____

GOAL (diagnosis)   Ideas to improve

PROGRESS NOTES

DATE: _____   NAME: _____

GOAL (diagnosis)   Ideas to improve

PROGRESS NOTES

DATE: _____   NAME: _____

GOAL (diagnosis)   Ideas to improve

PROGRESS NOTES

DATE: _____   **NAME:** _____

GOAL (diagnosis)   **Ideas to improve**

PROGRESS NOTES

DATE: _____   NAME: _____

GOAL (diagnosis)   Ideas to improve

PROGRESS NOTES

DATE: _____   NAME: _____

GOAL (diagnosis)   Ideas to improve

PROGRESS NOTES

DATE: _____   NAME: _____

GOAL (diagnosis)   Ideas to improve

PROGRESS NOTES

DATE: _____   NAME: _____

GOAL (diagnosis)   Ideas to improve

PROGRESS NOTES

DATE: _____   NAME: _____

GOAL (diagnosis)   Ideas to improve

PROGRESS NOTES

DATE: _____   NAME: _____

GOAL (diagnosis)   Ideas to improve

PROGRESS NOTES

DATE: _____   NAME: _____

GOAL (diagnosis)   Ideas to improve

PROGRESS NOTES

DATE: _____   NAME: _____

GOAL (diagnosis)   Ideas to improve

PROGRESS NOTES

DATE: _____   NAME: _____

GOAL (diagnosis)   Ideas to improve

PROGRESS NOTES

DATE: _____   NAME: _____

GOAL (diagnosis)   Ideas to improve

PROGRESS NOTES

DATE: _____   NAME: _____

GOAL (diagnosis)   Ideas to improve

PROGRESS NOTES

DATE: _____   NAME: _____

GOAL (diagnosis)   Ideas to improve

PROGRESS NOTES

DATE: _____   **NAME:** _____

GOAL (diagnosis)   **Ideas to improve**

PROGRESS NOTES

DATE: _____   NAME: _____

GOAL (diagnosis)   Ideas to improve

PROGRESS NOTES

DATE: _____   NAME: _____

GOAL (diagnosis)   Ideas to improve

PROGRESS NOTES

DATE: _____   NAME: _____

GOAL (diagnosis)   Ideas to improve

PROGRESS NOTES

DATE: _____   NAME: _____

GOAL (diagnosis)   Ideas to improve

PROGRESS NOTES

DATE: _____   NAME: _____

GOAL (diagnosis)   Ideas to improve

PROGRESS NOTES

DATE: _____   **NAME:** _____

GOAL (diagnosis)   **Ideas to improve**

PROGRESS NOTES

DATE: _____   NAME: _____

GOAL (diagnosis)   Ideas to improve

PROGRESS NOTES

DATE: _____   **NAME:** _____

GOAL (diagnosis)   **Ideas to improve**

PROGRESS NOTES

DATE: _____   NAME: _____

GOAL (diagnosis)   Ideas to improve

PROGRESS NOTES

DATE: _____   **NAME:** _____

GOAL (diagnosis)   **Ideas to improve**

PROGRESS NOTES

DATE: _____   NAME: _____

GOAL (diagnosis)   Ideas to improve

PROGRESS NOTES

DATE: _____   **NAME:** _____

GOAL (diagnosis)   **Ideas to improve**

PROGRESS NOTES

DATE: _____   NAME: _____

GOAL (diagnosis)   Ideas to improve

PROGRESS NOTES

DATE: _____   NAME: _____

GOAL (diagnosis)   Ideas to improve

PROGRESS NOTES

DATE: _____   NAME: _____

GOAL (diagnosis)   Ideas to improve

PROGRESS NOTES

DATE: _____   NAME: _____

GOAL (diagnosis)   Ideas to improve

PROGRESS NOTES

DATE: _____   NAME: _____

GOAL (diagnosis)   Ideas to improve

PROGRESS NOTES

DATE: _____   NAME: _____

GOAL (diagnosis)   Ideas to improve

PROGRESS NOTES

DATE: _____   NAME: _____

GOAL (diagnosis)   Ideas to improve

PROGRESS NOTES

DATE: _____   **NAME:** _____

GOAL (diagnosis)   **Ideas to improve**

PROGRESS NOTES

DATE: _____   NAME: _____

GOAL (diagnosis)   Ideas to improve

PROGRESS NOTES

DATE: _____   NAME: _____

GOAL (diagnosis)   Ideas to improve

PROGRESS NOTES

DATE: _____   NAME: _____

GOAL (diagnosis)   Ideas to improve

PROGRESS NOTES

DATE: _____   NAME: _____

GOAL (diagnosis)   Ideas to improve

PROGRESS NOTES

DATE: _____   NAME: _____

GOAL (diagnosis)   Ideas to improve

PROGRESS NOTES

DATE: _____   NAME: _____

GOAL (diagnosis)   Ideas to improve

15846520R00238

Made in the USA
Lexington, KY
21 June 2012